THE SUPERMALE

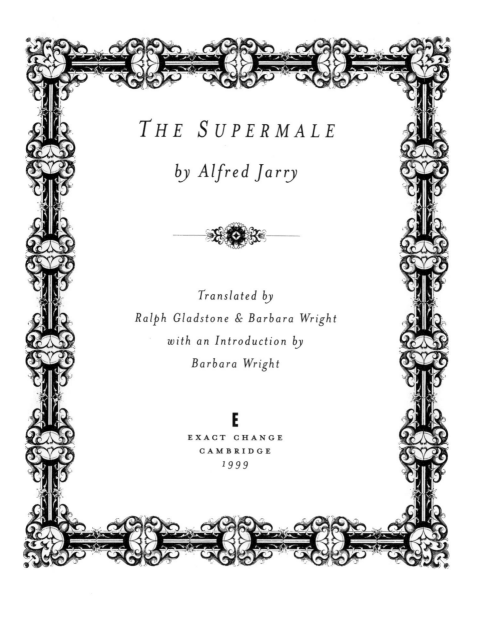

THE SUPERMALE

by Alfred Jarry

Translated by
Ralph Gladstone & Barbara Wright
with an Introduction by
Barbara Wright

E

EXACT CHANGE
CAMBRIDGE
1999

Cover illustration: *La santé par le sport* by Max Ernst, 1920
Reproduced by permission of The Menil Collection, Houston

Exact Change books are edited by Damon Krukowski
and designed by Naomi Yang

Exact Change
5 Brewster Street
Cambridge, MA 02138
www.exactchange.com

Printed on acid-free recycled paper

Alfred Jarry is still, outside France, mainly known as the author of the "scandalous" play *Ubu Roi*, which was probably the first example of the "Theater of the Absurd." It was indeed *Ubu* that shot Jarry, at the age of twenty-three, into instant notoriety in the fin-de-siècle "belle époque" Paris of 1896, but *Ubu* represents only one aspect of his multifarious talents.

Born in Laval, which is near enough to Brittany for him to have boasted of being a Breton, Jarry was a brilliant student at the lycées of Laval and Rennes, and went to Paris in 1891 to study at the lycée Henri IV in order to prepare entry to the prestigious college École Normale Supérieure. Though he did well at Henri IV, where he studied philosophy (with Bergson), Latin, Greek, history, French, mathematics, cosmography, and modern languages, he failed in three successive years to get a place at the École Normale (which, it must be said, only had room for twenty-four new students each year from the whole of France). With characteristic obstinacy Jarry put his name down for a fourth attempt, but he withdrew his candidature at the last moment, for by now — 1894 — he was already a well-known figure in the world of avant-garde literature. He had written poems, stories and criticism for little reviews; he had three times won competitions organized by the *Écho de Paris;* he was already a contributor to the influential *Revue Blanche* and, more importantly, to the Symbolist review *Le Mercure de France,* whose director, Alfred Vallette, and his wife, the novelist Rachilde, were to become his life-long friends and supporters.

It is interesting to discover that Jarry, who throughout his short life (he died when he was thirty-four) was notorious for his consciously provocative and outrageous behavior, had during his early student days at Henri IV earned a reputation with at least some of his contemporaries for being shy, well behaved, conscientious, and studious. He was soon to shed the first three characteristics, but studious he was to remain for the rest of his life. Already while following the grueling Henri IV program he was reading widely on a tremendous variety of other subjects at the Bibliothèque Sainte-Geneviève; he was interested in all branches of science (and at one time actually considered following a scientific career), but at the same time he was attracted to Rosicrucianism and other esoteric arts then popular. He was also fascinated by heraldry. Nor did he disdain sports: he was a passionate and skillful fisherman and oarsman, a good fencer, and an ardent cyclist. In 1896 he acquired a "Clément luxe" bicycle, the latest, fastest, and most elegant model. (It cost the fabulous sum of 525 francs, of which the unfortunate dealer was never paid more than a few derisory installments.)

The 1890s saw the heyday of Symbolism; Jarry was one of its staunchest defenders, and his early writings were profoundly influenced by the movement. His first book, *Les Minutes de Sable Mémorial,* a gallimaufry of Symbolist poems, fragments from *Ubu* and from other works in progress, was published in 1894 by Alfred Vallette under the *Mercure* imprint. He was also a partisan of the modern painters of the time — Gauguin (with whom he stayed at Pont Aven), Van Gogh, Bonnard, Vuillard, Émile Bernard. Among the Symbolist writers and polemicists, Mallarmé, Remy de Gourmont, Henri de Régnier, and Marcel Schwob were his friends, but Jarry's tastes were always catholic; he was, for instance, one of the first to recognize the gifts of the Douanier Rousseau. (They had been friends for some time: when Jarry was thrown out of his slum room in 1897 it was the Douanier who sheltered him in his own equally slummy room around the corner, in the Avenue du Maine.)

In 1896, though, Jarry had become the secrétaire-régisseur of the avant-garde Théâtre de l'Oeuvre, then in the forefront of the Symbolist and anarchist movements and directed by the young Lugné-Poe. This gave him the chance to persuade Lugné-Poe to stage his *Ubu Roi,* an event which was to be the turning point in his life. The scandal of its two first performances in December 1896 has been compared to that of the "battle" of Victor Hugo's *Hernani* nearly a century earlier, which marked the beginning of the literary rebellion that was later consolidated into the Romantic movement. *Ubu Roi* stemmed from a corporate drama, *Les Polonais,* which Jarry and his fellow students at the Rennes lycée had written with the cruel aim of ridiculing their unfortunate physics professor, M. Hébert, known as Le Père Ébé. Jarry made *Les Polonais* his own, changed, adapted, and developed it, and later wrote the sequels *Ubu Enchaîné* and *Ubu Cocu.*

Ubu, with his cupidity, stupidity, ferocity, and cowardice, symbolized Jarry's revolt against the accepted values of the time. Jarry did not make Ubu the embodiment of "vice" in order to present a "vile" character but, on the contrary, in order to show up all the establishment figures around him — kings, nobles, generals, magistrates; Ubu's very presence strips them of their false pretensions and sentiments. The only commoners in the Ubu plays are peasants, whom Ubu robs as everyone else has always robbed them, but he does it in a more open and dynamic way, and totally without hypocrisy. Jarry's methods were mystification, surprising associations, gross exaggeration, and a wild humor which, as a method, remains humor even when it is no longer funny and has even perhaps become tragic; his is a sophisticated kind of satire which appears deceptively simple. The audience at the Théâtre de l'Oeuvre, who were representative of the literary and other elites, naturally had no wish to be confronted on the stage with what Jarry called their "ignoble otherself," and they and most critics greeted the play with horror and uproar.

Catulle Mendès was one of the few critics who was prepared to see clearly: "A new type has emerged," he wrote. "Père Ubu exists... He will become a popular legend of base instincts, rapacious and violent; and Monsieur Jarry, who I hope is destined for a more worthy celebrity, will have created an infamous mask."

Jarry now had only eleven more years to live. After the sensation of *Ubu Roi* his life style became more and more eccentric, and his "self-inflicted nightmare" began in earnest. He identified himself with Ubu to the extent of actually referring to himself as "le Père Ubu" and using the royal "we"; he amused himself by insulting and terrorizing the bourgeoisie he so despised (often with a loaded revolver; he was an excellent shot). And though he always retained the affection and esteem of such friends as the Vallettes, he was already on the downward path toward self-destruction. If there was no difference between life and literature, if nothing was sacred and everything was absurd and meaningless, the logical conclusion was self-annihilation.

He dissipated the small personal fortune that had come to him on the death of his parents, and lived for the last ten years of his life in a squalid room that was just high enough to allow him — he was only a little over five feet tall — to stand up. (A rapacious landlord had divided one small apartment into four, vertically and horizontally. History doesn't seem to relate who lived in the other three midget dwellings.) He neglected himself, didn't eat, drowned himself in absinthe, and later became addicted to ether (which was cheaper). He died at thirty-four, his last request being for a toothpick.

Against the tragic negativity of his personal life, though, Jarry almost to the end practiced every sort of positive artistic creativity. He had a great influence on slightly younger writers such as Apollinaire, André Salmon, and Max Jacob, and also on Picasso, who collected some of his manuscripts. The Cubists felt an affinity with him, and André Breton recognized him as a precursor of Surrealism. Among Jarry's other talents were painting, drawing, and engraving. He also translated works that he particularly admired: Coleridge's *Ancient Mariner; Scherz, Satire, Ironie und tiefere Bedeutung* from the German of that other poète maudit, Christian-Dietrich Grabbe; and *Pope Joan,* from the Greek of Emmanuel Rhoïdes. At least twenty items of original writing are to be found in his bibliography, among which perhaps the most important is *Les Gestes et opinions du Docteur Faustroll, pataphysicien.* This "neo-scientific novel" was not published in its entirety in French until some years after Jarry's death. It first appeared in an English translation by Simon Watson Taylor in *The Selected Works of Alfred Jarry* (Grove Press, 1965), jointly edited by Watson Taylor and Roger Shattuck, the American Jarry scholar.* Shattuck writes in his introduction:

"*Faustroll* reveals its enigmatic qualities most clearly in contrast to *Ubu Roi, Ubu Enchaîné,* and *Ubu Cocu.* In the nine-

---

*Simon Watson Taylor's translation, together with the introduction by Roger Shattuck quoted below, has been reprinted by Exact Change as *Exploits & Opinions of Doctor Faustroll, Pataphysician.*

ties Ubu's freewheeling and adolescent nihilism was received with a raucous mixture of hoots and cheers in the auditorium as in the press. Yet it was received. *Faustroll,* even though a few fragments appeared in the *Mercure de France* in May, 1895, encountered only silence and uneasy rejection by the two editors most devoted to Jarry's work. This time he appeared to have attempted too much. In a grotesque symmetry, *Faustroll* moves in the opposite direction from the *Ubu* plays and forms their complement. Beneath the highly congested surface, and in spite of its desultory structure, one senses in *Faustroll* the search for a new reality, a stupendous effort to create out of the ruins Ubu had left behind a new system of values — the world of Pataphysics. Beneath the double talk and ellipsis, its formal definition seems to mean that the virtual or imaginary nature of things as glimpsed by the heightened vision of poetry or science or love can be seized and lived as real. This is the ultimate form of 'authentic enactment.'"

It was in *Faustroll* that Jarry elaborated his "science" of Pataphysics, the science that lies behind all his thinking. Among other "formal definitions" of Pataphysics, we have:*

Pataphysics is the science of the realm beyond metaphysics; or, Pataphysics lies as far beyond metaphysics as metaphysics lies beyond physics — in one direction or another.

---

*The following definitions are drawn from Roger Shattuck's essay, "Superliminal Note," published as the introduction to the "What is 'Pataphysics?" number of the *Evergreen Review* (May/June 1960), and later reprinted (in nine languages) by the Collège de 'Pataphysique as, "On the Threshold of 'Pataphysics."

Pataphysics is the science of the particular, of laws governing exceptions.

Pataphysics is the science of imaginary solutions.

For Pataphysics, all things are equal.

In December 1948 an assorted group of professors and intellectuals, who considered Jarry to be one of the most neglected of great French writers, founded in Reims the College of Pataphysics. The college has produced a series of scholarly magazines and publications centered upon Jarry and his ideas, and has published many of his hitherto unknown works. At the same time it has continued his spirit of humorous and erudite mystification and his cold, clear analysis of received ideas, in whatever quarter they may be found. It has upset quite a few members of the present-day French establishment, who never know whether to take the college seriously or not. It has adopted (and adapted) Jarry's *Almanach du Père Ubu* as its own perpetual calendar: Jarry's birth date, September 8, 1873, is the first of the month of Absolu; we are now in the one hundred and fourth year of the Pataphysical Era and I am writing this, believe it or not, on the second day of Pédale, 104, the fête of S. André Marcueil, ascète cycliste. The college has also created its own hierarchy, which includes not a few of those upon whom the "vulgar" world has also thrust greatness, as for instance Ionesco, Jacques Prévert, René Clair, Marcel Duchamp, Dubuffet, Michel Leiris, and Raymond Queneau. Roger Shattuck is the Proveditor-

General Propagator for the Islands and the Americas, Regent (by Transseant Susception) of the Chair of Applied Mateology, GMOGG. Even I am a regent: as a reward for my translation of *Ubu Roi,* I was made Regent of Shakespearian Zozology.

The Supermale does not talk in so many words about Pataphysics, but the whole book is imbued with that science. The key word in the first definition of Pataphysics that I quoted is "beyond," and the essence of the Supermale is that he goes beyond everything hitherto imaginable. He is also very much the "particular," the "exception," and as for an "imaginary solution"... The book was published in 1902, but Jarry set it in 1920, a date very much in the future for him — so much in the future, in fact, that he didn't live to see it. *The Supermale,* like *Faustroll,* brings together most of the elements of Jarry's manifold talents and interests: poetry, classical learning, science, fantasy, imagination, comedy, and humor. It even reflects his hobbies — Elson's skill with a revolver, and the very idea of a bicycle as an inanimate hero — but more importantly, as with *Faustroll, The Supermale* is obsessed with the potentialities of man and what he considers to be his limitations; with the idea of extending frontiers, pushing the possible to the limits of the imaginable, discovering what might be done by will power to liberate and control the energy of the universe.

André Marcueil is one of a long line of Jarry's heroes with whom he identified himself — supermen so superior to ordinary mortals that they become God. In *Faustroll*

(Jarry's "spiritual autobiography"*), Dr. Faustroll is a man-god who survives his own death. In *L'Amour Absolu,* whose hero is called Emmanuel Dieu, "Jarry makes himself God"**; in *César-Antechrist* he asserts that one has to be God in order to be a man, and in *L'Amour en Visites* he writes: "Man must amuse himself in the image of his creator. God has amused himself savagely ever since he has been God, only he isn't going to amuse himself much longer, because I am here. A good God always dethrones another God."

A god, perhaps, in his imagination (which he continually asserted was "real" life), but in what to other people is the real life of the here and now, Jarry was something less than godlike. And such were the contradictions of his character that when, after a complete physical breakdown in 1906, he thought he was dying, in spite of all his braggadocio and blasphemy, he not only received extreme unction, like any good Catholic, but also wrote to his friends to tell them of it. His megalomania was a mask for a great deal of misery, but his works have already guaranteed him that "worthy celebrity" that Catulle Mendès predicted for him eighty years ago.

BARBARA WRIGHT
1977

---

*Roger Shattuck, introduction to *Exploits & Opinions of Doctor Faustroll, Pataphysician.*
**Noël Arnaud, *Alfred Jarry: d'Ubu roi au Docteur Faustroll* (Paris: La Table Ronde, 1974).

THE SUPERMALE

THE HIGHEST BIDDER

"The act of love is of no importance, since it can be performed indefinitely."

All eyes were turned upon the perpetrator of this absurdity.

The conversation of André Marcueil's guests at the Château de Lurance that evening had come round to the subject of love as being, by common consent, the most appropriate, seeing that there were ladies present, and as being also the subject most likely, even in that September of 1920, to avoid tedious discussion about the Dreyfus Affair.

Among those present were the celebrated American chemist William Elson, a widower, with his daughter Ellen; the millionaire engineer, electrical expert, and manufacturer of automobiles and aircraft, Arthur Gough, with his wife; General Sider; Senator de Saint-Jurieu with his baroness, Pusice-Euprépie de Saint-Jurieu; Cardinal Romuald; the actress Henriette Cyne, and Doctor Bathybius.

These diverse and notable figures could easily have reinvigorated the commonplace, pushing it effortlessly toward paradox, merely by each expressing his own original thoughts, but their good manners soon reduced the remarks of these celebrated wits to the polished insignificance of society conversation.

And so this unexpected statement had much the same effect as that, which even to this day has been insufficiently analyzed, of a stone cast into a frog pond; momentary turmoil, followed by universal interest.

It might very likely have produced a different result: smiles, but by mischance it had been uttered by the host.

André Marcueil's face, like his aphorism, left a sort of gap in the assembly; not, however, by its singularity, but — if it is possible to couple the two words — by its characteristic insignificance. It was as pale as his starched shirt fronts, and would almost have merged into the woodwork, pale in the electric light, had it not been for the inky fringe of his collar-fashion beard, and for his longish hair which he had curled, probably to conceal incipient baldness. His eyes were most likely black, but were certainly weak, for he concealed them behind the tinted lenses of gold-rimmed pince-nez. Marcueil was thirty years old, and of medium height, though by adopting a pronounced stoop he seemed to take pleasure in making himself seem even shorter than he was. His wrists were thin, and so hairy as to resemble exactly his frail, black-silk-encased ankles. His wrists and ankles alike gave rise to the supposition that he must be remarkably weak in his entire person, to judge at least by what one could see of it. He spoke slowly and in a deep voice, as though anxious to spare his breath. Had he owned a hunting permit his description would no doubt have read: chin: round; face: oval; nose: average; mouth: average; height: average... In fact Marcueil embodied so absolutely the average man that his very ordinariness became extraordinary.

The remark took on a pitifully ironic significance, whispered like a breath from the mouth of this little man. He obviously did not know what he was saying. He was not known to keep a mistress, and presumably the state of his health precluded love.

A "chilled silence" fell, and someone was about to change the subject when Marcueil continued:

"I am quite serious, gentlemen."

"I thought," minced the no longer youthful Pusice-Euprépie de Saint-Jurieu, "that love was a sentiment."

"Perhaps so, madam," replied Marcueil. "All we need is to agree on... what we mean by... a sentiment."

"It is an impression upon the soul," the cardinal hastened to say.

"I read something of the sort in my youth, in the spiritual philosophers," added the senator.

"An enfeebled sensation," said Bathybius. "Praised by the English Associationists!"

"I am nearly of the same opinion as the doctor," said Marcueil. "It is an attenuated act, most likely; that is, not quite an act; or better still, a potential act."

"If you accept that definition," said Saint-Jurieu, "would the completed act exclude love?"

Henriette Cyne yawned ostentatiously.

"Certainly not," said Marcueil.

The ladies thought they ought to be preparing to blush behind their fans, or to hide behind those fans the fact that they were not blushing.

"Certainly not," he continued, "if each completed act is followed by another act that remains... sentimental in this respect — that it will only be completed sometime later."

This time several people could not prevent themselves smiling.

Their host, amused by the unfolding of his paradox, seemed to grant them full license.

It is a fact that has often been observed that it is the weakest people who are the most concerned — in imagination — with physical exploits.

The doctor alone objected coldly:

"But the repetition of a vital act causes the death of the tissues, or their intoxication, which we call fatigue."

"Repetition produces habit — and ability," retorted Marcueil with equal gravity.

"Hurray! Training!" cried Arthur Gough.

"Mithridatism," said the chemist.

"Exercise," added the general.

"Present... arms! One, two, three!" quipped Henriette Cyne.

"Quite so, mademoiselle," Marcueil concluded, "if you will only keep counting until you exhaust the infinite series of numbers."

"Or, to be brief, of human capacities," interjected Mrs. Arabella Gough with her charming lisp.

"Human capacities have no limits, madam," asserted André Marcueil calmly.

All the smiles had vanished, despite this new opportunity the orator was affording for them. Such a theorem revealed that Marcueil was driving at something. But what? Everything about his appearance proclaimed that he was less capable than anyone of launching himself upon the perilous path of personal example.

But their expectations were disappointed. He let it go at that, as though peremptorily closing the discussion with a universal truth.

The doctor was irritated, and it was again he who broke the silence:

"Is what you mean to say that there are organs that work and rest almost simultaneously, and give the illusion of never stopping?..."

"The heart; let's remain sentimental," said William Elson.

"...until death," concluded Bathybius.

"That is quite long enough to represent an infinite amount of work," remarked Marcueil. "The number of diastoles and systoles in a human lifetime, or even in a single day, surpasses all imaginable figures."

"But the heart is a very simple system of muscles," the doctor corrected him.

"My motors stop sure enough when they run out of fuel," said Arthur Gough.

"One might conceive," ventured the chemist, "of a fuel for the human machine that could indefinitely delay muscular and nervous fatigue, repairing it as it is spent. I recently invented something of the sort..."

"What," said the doctor, "your Perpetual Motion Food* again? You are forever talking about it, and we never get to see any. I thought you were supposed to have sent some to our friend..."

"What was that?" asked Marcueil. "You forget, my friend, that one of my several infirmities is that I don't understand English."

"Perpetual Motion Food," repeated the chemist.

"The name is intriguing," said Bathybius. "What do you think of it, Marcueil?"

"You know I never take medicines... even though my best friend is a doctor," Marcueil hastened to add, bowing slightly toward Bathybius.

"He's making altogether too much of the fact that he knows nothing, doesn't want to know anything, and is anemic, the dog," muttered the doctor to himself.

"I should think that sort of chemistry would be rather unnecessary," continued Marcueil, addressing William Elson. "Complex nervous and muscular systems enjoy absolute rest, it seems to me, while their 'counterpart' works. We know that, for a bicyclist, each leg in turn rests, and even benefits from a massage that is automatic, and as restorative as any embrocation, while the other leg is doing its work..."

"Well now, and where did you learn that?" asked Bathybius. "Surely you don't ride a bicycle?"

"I am not very well suited to physical exercise, my

---

*In English in the original

friend," answered Marcueil. "I am not nearly spry enough."

"Bah! This is just cussedness," muttered the doctor once more. "He just refuses to know anything, both in the physical and the moral field... But why? True enough he doesn't look very well."

"You may judge the effects of my Perpetual Motion Food without subjecting yourself to the trouble of tasting it, and while simply remaining a spectator at a physical performance," said William Elson to Marcueil. "The day after tomorrow a race starts in which a bicycle team will be fed on it exclusively. If you will do me the honor of attending the finish..."

"What will the team be racing against?" asked Marcueil.

"Against a train," said Arthur Gough, "and I dare say my locomotive will reach undreamed-of speeds."

"Really? And are they to race far?" Marcueil inquired.

"Ten thousand miles," replied Arthur Gough.

"Sixteen thousand and ninety-three kilometers," explained William Elson.

"Large numbers like that don't really mean anything;" remarked Henriette Cyne.

"Farther than from Paris to the Sea of Japan," Arthur Gough clarified. "Since there is not room enough between Paris and Vladivostok for our ten thousand miles exactly, we have put in a curve two thirds of the way down the track, between Irkutsk and Stryensk."

"And so, in fact," said Marcueil, "we shall see the finish in Paris, which is all to the good. How many hours will it take?"

"We estimate five days' traveling time," replied Arthur Gough.

"That's a long time," remarked Marcueil.

The chemist and the engineer suppressed a shrug of their shoulders at this observation, which revealed all the shortcomings of their host.

Marcueil corrected himself:

"I mean, it would be more interesting to follow the race than to wait at the finish."

"We are taking two sleeping cars along," said William Elson, "which are at your disposal. The only passengers, apart from the crew, will be my daughter, myself, and Gough."

"My wife is not going," said Gough. "She's too nervous."

"I don't know whether I am nervous too," said Marcueil, "but I'm always sure to be seasick on a train, and to be afraid of accidents, too. In the absence of my sedentary self, let my best wishes accompany you."

"But you will at least see the finish?" insisted Elson.

"*At least* the finish, I will try," acquiesced Marcueil, stressing his words in a bizarre fashion.

"Just what is your Perpetual Motion Food?" inquired Bathybius of the chemist.

"I can't reveal that, of course, except that it has a strychnine and alcohol base," replied Elson.

"Strychnine in sizeable doses is a stimulant, as is well known, but alcohol? For training racers? You're pulling my leg; I'm not prepared to accept your theories," exclaimed the doctor.

"We're straying from the heart of the matter," commented Mrs. Gough.

"Gentlemen, a little higher," replied Marcueil in his blank voice, with no apparent impertinence.

"Human capacities in love may well be infinite," went on Mrs. Gough, "but as one of these gentlemen was saying a moment ago, it is a matter of definition. Now it would be interesting to know at precisely what point in the infinite series of numbers the male sex places infinity."

"I have read that Cato the Elder placed it as high as two," jested Saint-Jurieu, "but he meant once in the winter and once in the summer."

"He was sixty years old, my dear," observed his wife, "don't forget that."

"That's a lot," murmured the general absent-mindedly, though no one could make out which of the two figures he was dreaming of.

"In the *Labors of Hercules*," said the actress, "King Lysius offers the hero his thirty virgin daughters for a single night, and sings, to the music of Claude Terrasse:

"Thirty! — that's just a game to such as you,
I crave your pardon that I bring so few!"

"But if it's sung —" said Mrs. Gough.

"Then it's not worth..." said Saint-Jurieu.

"...*doing*," interrupted André Marcueil. "Besides, are we sure that the number was only thirty?"

"If my classical memory may be trusted," said the doctor, "the authors of the *Labors of Hercules* seem to have humanized mythology. I think Diodorus of Sicily actually states: *Herculem una nocte quinquaginta virgines mulieres reddidisse.*"

"Which means?" asked Henriette.

"Fifty virgins," explained the senator.

"The same Diodorus, my dear doctor, mentions a certain Proculus," said Marcueil.

"Yes," said Bathybius, "the man who had entrusted to him a hundred Sarmatian maidens and to 'constuprate' them, says the text, required only a fortnight."

"It's in the *Treatise on the Vanity of Science,* Chapter III," Marcueil confirmed. "But two weeks! Why not at three months' maturity?"

"The *Thousand and One Nights,*" quoted William Elson in his turn, "contends that the third Calender, a king's son, knew, forty times apiece, forty young girls in forty nights."

"These are Oriental imaginings," Arthur Gough thought he should explain.

"Another Oriental article which is no article of faith, albeit enshrined in the sacred Koran," said Saint-Jurieu, "has Mohammed boast of possessing the virility of sixty men."

"That doesn't mean he could make love sixty times," observed the senator's wife with some show of wit.

"Is he the highest bidder?" asked the general. "I think we must be playing auction manille. And this game is even more frivolous. I pass."

There was an outcry:

"Oh! General!"

"But surely, when you were in Africa?..." Henriette Cyne whispered insidiously under the general's goatee.

"In Africa?" said the general. "That's different. But I wasn't there during the war. There may be a rape or two, in wartime…"

"One or two? That's a number, that's even two numbers, but which one is it?" asked Saint-Jurieu.

"Manner of speaking! Let me continue," the general went on. "So I've only been in Africa in peacetime. And what is the duty of a French soldier abroad in peacetime? Is it to act like a savage? Or is it not rather to bring civilization with him, and particularly that which is most seductive in that civilization — French gallantry? So that when the harems of Algiers learn that our officers are coming it gives them a change from those uncouth Arabs, who know nothing of refined manners, and they exclaim: 'Oh! Here come the Frenchmen! Now we'll see some…'"

"General, I have a young daughter," said William Elson with some severity, and just in time.

"But it seems to me," said the general, "that our conversation so far, with all these figures…"

"Are you talking business, gentlemen?" inquired the young American girl with more than praiseworthy naïveté.

William Elson motioned to her to withdraw.

"We should have started by consulting the doctor, ladies," remarked Mrs. Gough, "instead of listening so patiently to all these nasty technicalities."

"I once observed," said Bathybius, "an idiot in the hospital at Bicêtre — he was an epileptic too — who, all his life, and he is still alive, has given himself up almost uninterruptedly to sexual acts. But… in solitude, which explains a lot."

"How horrible," said several ladies.

"I mean, his cerebral stimulation explains everything," the doctor went on.

"Then is it women who inhibit men?" asked Henriette.

"I told you in the first place that he is an idiot, mademoiselle."

"But... you were talking about his... cerebral capacities! So he couldn't have been so much of an idiot after all," said Henriette.

"Besides, it isn't the brain but the medulla which is the center of those emotions," replied Bathybius.

"His medulla had genius," said Marcueil.

"But... since we are not in Bicêtre... what about people outside?" inquired Mrs. Gough.

"According to the medical profession, human capacity may reach from nine to twelve, at the most, in twenty-four hours, and then only in exceptional cases," stated Bathybius.

"The apostle of unlimited human capabilities now has the floor, to reply to human science," said William Elson to his host with friendly irony.

"I regret," said André Marcueil in the slightly mocking, expectant silence that ensued, "I regret that I am unable, without falsification, to have my convictions conform to worldly opinions and to science. Scientists, as you have just heard, are of a mind with those savages in the heart of Africa who, in order to express any number greater than five — whether it be six or a thousand — wave their ten fingers in the air and say: 'Many, many.' But I really believe that

...that's just a game,

not only to wed the thirty or fifty virgin daughters of King Lysius, but to beat the record set by that Indian 'so celebrated by Theophrastus, Pliny and Athenaeus' who, Rabelais reports after these authors, 'with the aid of a certaine Herb, did it in one Day threescore Times and ten, and More.'"

"He scored three times in ten?" joked the general, an inveterate punster.

"*Septuageno coitu durasse libidinem contactu herbae cujusdam,*" quoted Bathybius, wishing to interrupt him. "I think the phrase is from Pliny, after Theophrastus."

"The author of the *Characters?*" asked Saint-Jurieu.

"Oh no!" said the doctor. "The author of the *History of Plants* and the *Causes of Plants.*"

"Theophrastus of Eresus,"said Marcueil, "in the twentieth chapter of Book IX of his *History of Plants.*"

"With the aid of a certain herb?" reflected Elson, the chemist.

"*Herbae cujusdam,*" pontificated Bathybius, "*cujus nomen genusque non posuit.* But Pliny, in Book III, Chapter XXVIII, infers that it must be the marrowy substance in the branches of the tithymallum."

"That tells us a lot," said Mrs. Gough. "It's even more obscure than saying 'a certain herb.'"

"It's pleasanter to believe," said Marcueil, "that the

'certain herb' was added by some timorous copyist to cushion the reader's mind against what he judged too rude a shock."

"With or without the herb... in one day? I mean, just one day out of a man's life?" inquired Madame de Saint-Jurieu.

"What can be done on one day can, with all the more reason, be done every day," said Marcueil. "One grows accustomed... But if this man was very exceptional, it is indeed possible that he succeeded in confining it within the space of one day.... We may also suppose that he occupied his time in a like manner every day, and that he admitted spectators only once."

"An Indian?" mused Henriette Cyne. "A red man with a tomahawk and scalps, like in Fenimore Cooper?"

"No, my child," said Marcueil. "What we today call a Hindu. But the country is unimportant. I agree with you, Rabelais's phrase rings majestic: 'That Indian so celebrated by Theophrastus,' and it's a shame that he wasn't a real Indian, a Delaware or a Huron, so as to create your imaginary scene."

"A Hindu?" said the doctor. "True, if it were not so flagrantly incredible... India *is* the land of aphrodisiacs."

"Chapter XX of Book IX of Theophrastus of Eresus does in fact deal with aphrodisiacs," said Marcueil, becoming more animated, and his eyes flashing behind his pince-nez, "but I repeat that I believe that neither the drug nor the country is important, and that there would be all the more reason for a white man... But," he added, almost in an aside, "in a man from a strange country one would think of such prowess as less strange, less incredible, just because it does *seem* to be prowess!... In any case, *what one man has done, another man can do.*"

"Do you know who was the first to put your ruminations into words?" interrupted Mrs. Gough, who was well read.

"My...?"

"Exactly. Your sentence: 'what one man has done...'"

"Ah yes! but I wasn't thinking of that. That's to be found... well, of course," said Marcueil, "in the *Adventures of Baron Munchausen.*"

"I don't know that German," said the general.

"A colonel, general," whispered Mrs. Gough, "a colonel of red hussars — M. de Crac, in French."

"Oh, I get it; tall tales," said the general.

"Actually," said Madame de Saint-Jurieu to Marcueil, "it would have been impossible to insinuate more wittily that the Indian's record could only be beaten by... let me see... by that other redskin, or red hussar... with such an imagination!"

"So that is what you were driving at," added Henriette Cyne, " — and this is... where you have led us! You've closed the bidding most astutely, putting up as..."

"Highest bidder, go ahead and say it," said Saint-Jurieu.

"...someone to whom words cost nothing."

"All you need for that is a good loose tongue in your head," said the general.

"Like in Africa," said Henriette Cyne. "...But that was a silly thing for me to say."

"Gentlemen," said André Marcueil in a loud and ceremonious voice, "I believe that Colonel Baron Munchausen accomplished all that he claimed, and more."

"Then the bidding is still open?" inquired Mrs. Gough.

"This is becoming a bit tiresome," said Henriette Cyne.

"Come now, Marcueil," said Bathybius, "it's madness for a man to jump a pond on horseback, like your mythical baron, and then, midway to the other side, realizing he hadn't enough of a running start, to bring both himself and his horse back to his starting point, keeping himself up in the air merely by tugging on his own pigtail."

"It was the regulation in those days for all soldiers to wear their hair in a pigtail," interrupted Arthur Gough, with more erudition than appropriateness.

"...It's contrary to all physical laws," concluded Bathybius.

"There's nothing at all erotic about it," observed the senator vaguely.

"Nor impossible," retorted Marcueil.

"The gentleman is making fun of you," said Pusice-Euprépie to her husband.

"The baron made only one mistake," continued Marcueil, "and that was to relate his adventures *after* they had happened. I'll agree that it is somewhat strange that they *did* happen..."

"Somewhat!" exclaimed Henriette Cyne.

"Always supposing, of course, that they did," persisted the doctor, more calmly.

"If it is amazing that they happened," continued Marcueil imperturbably, "it is far less amazing that no one has ever believed him. And it's a good thing for the baron, too. Can you imagine the unbearable life a man who had seen such miracles would have led in an envious and malicious society? He would have been held responsible for every unexplained occurrence and every unpunished crime, the way witches were burned in olden times..."

"He would have been worshiped as God," said Ellen Elson, who had been called back by her father in deference to Baron Munchausen, a topic within a young lady's scope.

"Yet what freedom would he not have enjoyed," concluded Marcueil, "when you think that, even were he to commit crimes, universal disbelief would furnish him with an alibi!"

"And how is it," whispered Mrs. Gough, "that a little while ago you came so near to imitating the baron?"

"I did not relate anything *after* it happened, madame," said Marcueil, "since, unfortunately, I am not a person whose adventures are worth relating..."

"When *do* you tell, then?... *before?*" said Henriette Cyne.

"Tell what? and *before* what?" retorted Marcueil. "Come now, my dear, let's forget about these 'tall tales,' as our old friend the general so aptly terms them."

"Bravo, my dear fellow! Personally I only believe what's credible," said Sider approvingly.

Ellen Elson had drawn near to André Marcueil. He was stooping more than ever, his tufted beard made him seem even older, and his eyes seemed even more lackluster behind his pince-nez. In his impersonal evening clothes he seemed more grotesque and pathetic than a carnival mask. His face was hidden behind gold, glass, and hair; his very teeth were invisible behind the bushy drooping of his mustache. The maiden looked straight into the emptiness of the lenses of his pince-nez:

"I believe in the Indian," she murmured.

2

HIS HEART WAS NEITHER ON THE RIGHT
NOR ON THE LEFT

Except when he was being born, André Marcueil had at first had no contact with women, having been suckled by a goat, like any common Jove.

His father was dead, and up to the age of twelve he was raised by his mother and an older sister, passing his childhood in the most complete purity — if the Catholic faith is correct in terming purity the neglect, under pain of eternal suffering, of certain parts of the body.

At the age of twelve, still dressed in a loose-fitting smock and baggy knickerbockers, barelegged, he reached the solemn occasion of his first communion, and a tailor measured him for his first grown-up suit.

Little André could not quite understand why men — who are little boys over twelve — could no longer have their clothes made by a dressmaker... and he had never seen his penis.

He had never looked at himself in a mirror, except fully clothed and just about to go out. He thought he looked very ugly beneath the black trousers... and yet his playmates were so proud to be wearing them for the first time.

And what was more, the tailor also considered that the suit he had made him didn't fit very well. Something, below the belt, was making an unsightly bulge. The tailor whispered a few embarrassed words to Marcueil's mother, who blushed, and he vaguely perceived that he had some deformity — otherwise they wouldn't have been whispering in front of him — that he wasn't built like everyone else.

To be built like everyone else when he was grown up became an obsession with him.

"On the right," the tailor was saying mysteriously, like someone trying not to alarm a sick person. He no doubt thought that André's heart was on the right side.

But how could the heart be below the belt, even in a grownup?

The tailor stood perplexed, absently stroking the unwonted place with his thumb.

A new fitting the next day, after alterations and with new measurements, still produced no better fit.

For, between the *left* side and the *right,* there is one direction: *above.*

André's mother, like all *born* mothers, and even the other sort, wanted him to be a soldier. He swore that he would never again be the cause of a tailor's misfit, and calculated that he still had eight years left in which to correct his deformity before the shameful day when he would be obliged to reveal it before the conscription board.

As he remained assiduously chaste, he had no opportunity of learning whether it really was a deformity.

And when he did start going with girls — a ritual after taking the first part of the baccalaureate exam, and André was a year ahead of his class — the girls must have thought that, like all men, he was only a "man" at certain times, since he only went up to their rooms "for a moment."

For five years the prose of the Church haunted him:

Hostemque nostrum comprime...

For five years he took bromides and various other preparations and tried to exhaust himself by physical exercise, with the sole result of making himself exceedingly strong. He bound himself with thongs and slept on his stomach, pitting against the revolt of the Beast all the weight of his thick, athletic body.

Later, much later, he reflected that his efforts were perhaps only directed toward bridling a force that would never have revealed itself had it not had a destiny to accomplish.

Then, as a reaction, he had mistresses frantically, but neither he nor they took any pleasure in it: what for him was such a "natural" need was for them just a chore.

Being logical, he tried "unnatural" vices, just long enough to learn by experience what a gap lay between his strength and that of the rest of mankind.

His mother died, and among the family papers he found mention of a curious ancestor of his — more or less an ancestor, that is to say, as, being his maternal great-uncle, he had not contributed to his procreation. This relative had died before André's time and must have bequeathed him "his powers."

To this gentleman's death certificate was appended a physician's note which, in its ingenuous and incorrect style, we reproduce below. It was written in large black characters, like stitches of black thread on a bit of a shroud.

> Auguste-Louis Samson de Lurance, died 15th April, 1849, aged twenty-nine months and thirteen days, following upon a continuous green vomiting; having retained to his last breath a firmness of character far beyond his years, and a much too fertile [sic] imagination, added to which *his organism, overprecocious with relation to a certain development,* greatly contributing to the sorrow in which he has plunged his family for all eternity. May God have mercy on his soul!
>
> Dr. [illegible]

And now no monster or "human freak" hunted by a Barnum would have shown greater ingenuity in mingling with the crowd than André Marcueil. Conformity with the environment, or "mimesis," is one of the laws of self-preservation. There is less security in killing creatures weaker than oneself than there is in imitating them. It isn't the strongest who survive, for *they are alone.* There is great wisdom in modeling one's soul on that of one's janitor.

But why should Marcueil have felt the need at the same time to hide and to reveal himself? To deny his strength and to prove it? In order to test the fit of his mask, no doubt...

Perhaps, too, "the beast," unbeknownst to him, was beginning to emerge.

3

IT'S A FEMALE, BUT A VERY STRONG ONE

The guests were leaving.

Flowing out in a double row, their fur-wrapped silhouettes scattered to left and right of the lofty flight of steps.

Then, beneath the electric bulbs on the five iron posts set at irregular intervals down the driveway, came the movement of other lights, the click of horses' hoofs, the throbbing of several cars.

William Elson and his daughter, with the Goughs, moved off in a fantastic machine, scarlet and snorting, which disappeared in a few gliding bounds.

The various vehicles dispersed, and soon there was no other sound in front of the Château than the murmuring of the water flowing in the moat.

Lurance, which André Marcueil had inherited from his mother, had been built in the reign of Louis XIII, yet it seemed entirely natural for its huge, wrought-iron lampposts to be topped with arc-lamps, and for the water running in its grounds to propel the machinery to light them. And in the same way it seemed that the apparently endless driveways, whose broad radii led to all the horizons, had not merely been drawn for carriages to creep on, but that the architect, by some obscure premonitory flash of genius, had designed them, three hundred years in advance, for modern vehicles. There is certainly no reason for men to build enduring works if they do not vaguely imagine that these works must wait for some additional beauty with which they themselves cannot invest them, but which the future holds in store. Great works are not created great; they become so.

Lurance stands only a few kilometers southwest of Paris. Marcueil, seeming strangely irritated by the evening's conversation, concealed his desire for diversion behind an apparent solicitude for his guests: he insisted on driving the doctor and the general back to Paris himself.

Out of regard for the latter, who rebelled against new-fangled means of locomotion, and as there was no railway station near Lurance, Marcueil had had a coupé harnessed.

The weather was dry, clear, and cold. The road sounded like cardboard. In less than an hour they had reached the Étoile, and as it was not late — barely two in the morning — they went into an English bar.

"Hello, Mark Antony," said Bathybius to the barman.

"You seem to be an habitué," said the general.

"Is that hefty fellow legitimately entitled to enjoy a name so Shakespearianly Roman?" asked Marcueil.

"As a matter of fact, I have been told that he owes his historico-dramatical sobriquet to the remarkable solemnity with which he addresses his customers, a solemnity only comparable to Shakespeare's Mark Antony pronouncing his classic speech before Caesar's tomb. And his customers — jockeys, trainers, grooms, boxers, and the like — are all great lovers of a good fight, and very often stand in need of admonition."

"I hope we shall shortly have a sample; it might prove entertaining," said Marcueil.

They were served. The general drank stout, the doctor pale ale and Marcueil, decidedly a neutralist — except when he was amusing himself by propounding some paradoxical theorem — asked for an equal mixture of both brews, or half and half.

Despite the doctor's prediction, the bar was quiet; there was just enough conversation for its buzz to isolate theirs.

The doctor could not refrain from referring to Marcueil's earlier remarks at Lurance and gently pulling his leg about them. At heart he was somewhat piqued that his friend, even in jest, had not left the last word to his authority as a celebrated man of science.

"Now that we are among men," he said, "just one final remark about your myths: your Proculus, Hercules, and other heroes of fable did not feel that honor was satisfied with mere numerical exploits — which were no less fabulous than themselves. As you say, it was a game, and they played it hard. They had to have virgins, virgins, lots of virgins! While it is a medical fact that..."

"An experimental fact too — for I can see what you are going to say," interrupted the general.

"It is a medical fact that a virgin's embrace is difficult

and painful enough to prevent a man from either wishing to or being able to repeat it so frequently."

"Our chaste friend didn't think of that," said the general.

"The answer is simple," said Marcueil. "To take a historical — or, if you prefer to call it that, a mythological — example, we must obviously admit that Hercules, in his entire person, was superior to other men and also in... what shall I call it? in stature, in corpulence..."

"In caliber," said the general. "There are no ladies present, and anyway, it's a term in ordnance."

"Gynecologists speak of the measure of a *demivirgin*," continued Marcueil. "If we suppose that a lesser known practice admits of the measure of a *demigod*, then it follows that, for certain men, *all women are virgins*; some a little more, some a little less..."

"Don't let your conclusions overtake your premises, please," objected the doctor. "Don't say 'certain men,' but Hercules alone, if you must..."

"And he isn't here," the general thought fit to add, subtly.

"That's true, he isn't here — I was forgetting," said Marcueil in a rather strange tone. "Well then, let us take another example. Supposing a woman were to undergo a certain number of sexual assaults, say twenty-five, to take an arbitrary figure, as the professors have it..."

"'There's another star in my plate,' as the fairy story goes," muttered Bathybius, half-annoyed. "Enough of paradoxes, my dear fellow, please don't throw any more at us... if you want us to discuss things scientifically... although there's really nothing left to discuss."

"Twenty-five different men, just to humor you, doctor!"

"That's more natural," said the general.

"You mean, more scientific," corrected Bathybius, with unexpected gentleness.

"What would be the result, physiologically speaking? The affected tissues would contract..."

The doctor guffawed:

"No, certainly not. They would relax, and long before then."

"Where did you ever see such nonsense?" asked the general. "Is this another historical example?"

"It's still quite simple," continued Marcueil. "The woman known in history for having polished off more than twenty-five lovers in one day is..."

"Messalina," cried both the others.

"As you say. Now, there is one verse in Juvenal that no one has been able to translate, and if anyone has understood its true meaning, he hasn't dared publish it: the reader would have found it too absurd. This is the verse:

"...Tamen ultima cellam
Clausit, adhuc ardens RIGIDAE *tentigine vulvae."*

"There follows," said the doctor:

"Et lassata viris nec dum satiata recessit."

"We know," said Marcueil, "but modern criticism has proved that this verse, like all well-known verses, is an interpolation. Famous verses are like proverbs…"

"The wisdom of nations," said the general.

"You have guessed very subtly, general. And you will not disagree that nations arise from the gathering together in very great numbers of anyone who happens to come along…"

"Now really!" began the general.

"Listen though, general," said Bathybius; "this is becoming interesting. You were saying, Marcueil…?"

"That Messalina, leaving the arms of her twenty-five, or many more, lovers, is — and I am translating literally: 'still ardent' (I understand here: kept ardent by)… the words here become a bit coarse in French, even among men, and the rest of the Latin is self-explanatory."

"Yes, I understand the last word in the verse," said the general, ordering more stout.

"That isn't the important one," said Marcueil "but its adjective: RIGIDAE."

"I see no way to refute your interpretation," said Bathybius, "but… Messalina was just a nymphomaniac, that's all. This… hysterical example proves nothing at all."

"The only real women are Messalinas," murmured Marcueil inaudibly.

He went on:

"The organs of both sexes are made up of the same elements, are they not, doctor, with some differentiation?"

"Pretty well," replied the doctor. "And what are you getting at now?"

"At this, which is logical," said Marcueil: "that there is no reason why there should not be produced in men, once a certain figure is reached, the very same physiological phenomena as in a Messalina."

"You mean, *rigidi tentigo veretri?* But that's absurd, madly absurd," exclaimed the doctor. "It is the very absence of this indispensable phenomenon that will always prevent man from exceeding numerically what is in fact human capacity."

"Excuse me, doctor; it follows from my line of thought that this manifestation becomes permanent, and even more pronounced, as one moves beyond the limits of human strength toward numerical infinity; and that it is consequently advantageous to pass beyond as rapidly as is possible, or, if you prefer, as is conceivable."

Bathybius did not deign to answer. As for the general, he had lost interest in the conversation.

"Another question, doctor," Marcueil persisted. "Don't you agree that a man who, out of a million opportunities, seizes only one, is a moderate man? In sexual matters a continent man?"

The doctor looked at him.

"And doctor, I need not tell you that the number of opportunities afforded by nature for the act of reproduction, the number of ova within every woman, is..."

"Yes, eighteen million," said Bathybius dryly.

"Eighteen a day, surely there is nothing supernatural about that! Once in a million! And I am supposing a healthy man, but you must certainly have observed pathological cases?"

"Yes, indeed," said Bathybius testily: "priapism, satyr-iasis — but let's not judge by illnesses."

"And the influence of stimulants?"

"If we discount illnesses, let us discount aphrodisiacs."

"What about reserve foods, then, like alcohol? For it is really a superfood, something like beef, boiled eggs, or Gruyère cheese."

"You certainly do have your definitions," replied Bathybius, brightening suddenly. "You sound like our friend Elson. I see now that you haven't been serious for a minute. It's better that way. And besides, alcohol provokes sclerosis of the tissues."

"What?" asked the general.

"It hardens them," said Bathybius. "The arteries of alcoholics develop *sclerosis,* which ages them prematurely."

"Well then," said Marcueil, "...don't flinch, doctor: that 'indispensable phenomenon' you spoke of — could it be some form of sclerosis?"

"That's funny," said Bathybius, "but childish. Histologically speaking, it is idiotic. Experimentally, no one is less virile than an alcoholic. Alcohol may be handy for preserving children, but not, so far as I know, for begetting them!"

"What about someone under the influence of alcohol?" asked Marcueil.

"The effect doesn't last, and the danger with alcohol is that the reaction it produces exceeds its stimulation."

"You are a scientist, doctor, a great scientist, the greatest scientist of your time, which unfortunately implies that you are of your time. You are my venerable elder, doctor,

but do you know that our young generation is just starting
out, which means that its science is a fraction of a century
older than yours? The depressing reaction of alcohol, for
certain temperaments, actually *precedes* the stimulation!"

"It cannot precede," said the doctor. "It is bound to
follow a prior stimulation."

"What you are saying, then, and I am flattered by it, is
that I and others like me are the consequence of genera-
tions who have been overstimulated by the blood of meat
and the force of wine... the explosion that follows com-
pression! The fashion in definitions changes. A little
nearer the stone age, back in the nineteenth century, for
example, they would have called it 'thoroughbred'! Doctor,
it is time for the middle classes — I use the term for all the
sons of stale water and unwhite bread — to begin drinking
alcohol, if they want their posterity to equal us!"

"Are you against water?" asked the doctor, astonished.

"My dear Sangrado,* don't be alarmed: water isn't
particularly nauseating — not, at least, when you use it for
footbaths and enemas! To keep it for such uses is to do it
abundant honor! What would you think, then, of method-
ically increasing, in geometrical progression, I suppose, an
alcoholic's dose?" continued Marcueil, who seemed to be
finding great pleasure in teasing the doctor. "What would
you say to *alcoholizing an alcoholic?*"

"You're pulling my leg," muttered Bathybius, just as
he had answered William Elson.

---

*In Le Sage's picaresque romance *Gil Blas* (written between 1715 and 1735),
Doctor Sangrado was a quack physician who had two universal remedies — hot
water and bloodletting.

"I attach no importance to alcohol, any more than to any other stimulant," apologized Marcueil, "but I think it possible that a man capable of making love indefinitely might experience no difficulty in doing anything else indefinitely: drinking alcohol, digesting, spending his muscular forces, et cetera. Whatever the nature of the act, it is the same whether performed for the first time or the last, in the same way as, if the Highways Department hasn't made a mistake, the first kilometer of a road is equal to the last."

"Science has other convictions on that matter," said the doctor, who was getting annoyed. "Anywhere other than in the department of the impossible, which scientists do not admit, as they have no chair in it, energies can only develop if they are specialized — and even then not indefinitely! A wrestler is neither a stallion nor a thinker; the universal Hercules never has and never will exist, and as for the benefits of alcoholism: bulls drink only water!"

"Tell me, doctor," asked Marcueil as innocently as he could manage, "haven't you tried making them drink alcohol?"

But Bathybius didn't hear this: he had gone, slamming the door behind him. Actually he lived only a few steps away.

Then something happened:

Mark Antony shuddered, uncurled himself like a lion about to spring, drew himself up very gradually till he towered above his counter, stretched out his arms, coughed and said calmly: *"Order, please!"* in English.

That was all, and he sat down again.

The general, embarrassed by the doctor's ill humor, did his best to take André Marcueil's mind off it:

"Charming evening you gave us," he said. "You had a lot of people there."

André jumped, with a vehemence scarcely justified by the originality of the remark.

"By the way, general, it is to you I owe the honor of having received Mr. William Elson. He is a scientist of great merit."

"Pooh!" said the general, with the laudable intention, which was encouraged by the stout, of being modest, as if he had taken the compliment personally. "An unimportant chemist, let's not talk about it, my dear fellow. What's chemistry, between ourselves, my young friend? It's like a sort of photography, only you can never frame its prints."

"And..." continued André, hesitating, "...what about that girl, Miss Elson?"

"Pooh!" cried the general, who was now well launched on the art of declining praise, as if he were crossing Africa at a gallop, "Pooh! a little slip of a girl..."

He did not himself have the slightest idea what the end of his sentence was going to be, but one could imagine that it would be pejorative.

André Marcueil drew himself up, shaking the table and spilling the pewter mugs. Animated by a sudden burst of anger, he leaned his face close to the general's, and his pince-nez quivered as if it were about to be flung in the face of the general by the force of the looks Marcueil was giving him.

The general was flabbergasted, and even more so when he heard Marcueil hiss this baroque threat:

"General, I thought you had some... French gallantry in you! I ought to break you in two, but it's not worth it, you aren't strong enough! "

"Order, please! Order!" thundered Mark Antony's voice at the same time, drowning André Marcueil's.

The general imagined that he must have misheard; first because he saw no reason for Marcueil's anger, and secondly because he saw him spill the mugs. In order not to have to think too hard, he took it to mean: "This stout isn't strong enough."

"Barman!" he called.

And, to Marcueil:

"What will you have?"

But Marcueil paid, grasped the general by the arm, and hurried him off, first out of the bar, and then — signaling to his coupé to wait for them in the same place — in the direction of the Bois de Boulogne.

"But this isn't my way home," protested the general. "I live over by Saint-Sulpice!"

He thought: he must be drunk, though we've neither of us had very much. "Hey, old fellow — my young friend, I mean — we're going the wrong way. If you don't feel well — I can understand that, I was young myself, once — would you like me to take you back to your carriage?"

"You aren't strong enough," answered André Marcueil calmly.

"Huh? That's a good one," replied the other, shaking Marcueil's arm.

Marcueil stepped back.

"Where did he go?" The general looked around. "Talks about Hercules and gets floored by an old man's handshake. But where are you, my young friend? Is the night so dark, or have you turned into a Negro?"

He hummed:

> A Negro strong as Hercules
> A soldier once attacked...

"We're there," said Marcueil.

"Where?" wondered Sider. "Your house? My house?"

A white form rose up near them, like the milky globe of a night light. Two notes, like those of a cello, hooted. Further on, claws scuttled and a long, yapping sound was heard.

"Jackals?"

Then suddenly, and with the great facility pure souls possess for never being astonished, the general burst out laughing:

"When and how did we get in? It's closed at night! Now I see! You should have told me, my young friend, that you have an apartment in the zoo, unless it belongs to your mistress! It wouldn't surprise me, you're so eccentric! I ought to have guessed."

A macaw hoarsely cried the two syllables of its own name. The wild dogs growled from behind their bars, and the great white owl in his narrow cage stared at the two men with his blond eyes.

"I don't live here and I don't keep a mistress, but this

is the home of something strong enough for me to play with," said André Marcueil, slowly.

They walked along the enclosure. Big black forms sprang up, each one following them on the other side of its bars, and as they walked along new forms appeared.

"Well now! He really is drunk," said the general. "Funny place to look for pussy."

The elephant trumpeted in his house, and his windowpanes rattled.

"Is he going to box with the kangaroos? But they used to do that in the circus thirty years ago, that's nothing new! Come on, old fellow, let's go, it's quite enough that you climbed over the fence, the keepers will be after us: I know all about discipline!"

The sea-green aquarium rose up on their right. Marcueil turned to the left and the general breathed again, for there the animals' enclosures came to an end and he need no longer fear any more drunken foolhardiness from his companion.

"Look, I'm going to kill the beast," said Marcueil, very calmly.

"What beast? You're drunk, old man... my young friend," said the general.

"The beast," said Marcueil.

In front of them, compact in the moonlight, an iron thing was squatting, with things that looked like elbows on its knees, and armored shoulders without a head.

"The dynamometer!" exclaimed the general gleefully.

"I'm going to kill it," repeated Marcueil obstinately.

"My young friend," said the general, "when I was your

age, and even younger, when I was reading for the *École Polytechnique,* I often unhooked shop signs, unscrewed street urinals, stole milk bottles and locked drunks in hallways. But I haven't yet burgled a slot machine. You needn't deny it, you think it's a slot machine! Well, anyway, he's drunk... But be careful, there's nothing in it for you, my young friend!"

"It's full, it's full of strength, and full of numbers," André Marcueil was saying to himself.

"Well," the general condescended, "I don't mind helping you break the thing, but how? With our feet, with our fists? You don't want me to lend you my sword, do you, to cut it in half?"

"Break it? Oh, no," said Marcueil. "I want to *kill* it."

"Look out for the law, then, for *defacing a public monument!*" said the general.

"Kill... with a permit," said Marcueil. And he fumbled in his waistcoat pocket and pulled out a French ten-centime piece.

The dynamometer's slot glistened vertically.

"It's a female," said Marcueil gravely, "...but a very strong one."

The coin went in with a click; it was as if the massive machine were cunningly putting itself on guard.

André Marcueil seized the sort of iron armchair by both its arms and, with no apparent effort, pulled:

"Come, madame," he said.

His phrase ended in a terrible crashing of twisted steel, the broken springs writhed on the ground as if they were the beast's entrails; the dial grimaced and its needle raced madly around two or three times like a hunted creature looking for a way of escape.

"Let's move along," said the general. "The dog! Just to impress me he picked a worn-out instrument."

They were both very lucid now, although Marcueil had not thought to drop the two handles, which were like burnished *cestus*. They went out of the enclosure and up the avenue, toward the coupé.

Dawn was breaking, like the light from another world.

4

A LITTLE SLIP OF A GIRL

A woman coming in makes the same rustling sound as one undressing.

The next morning Miss Elson called on André Marcueil.

He had just had his breakfast, in secret, since, like a desperate consumptive or a healthy savage, he followed a diet of raw mutton. He had then proceeded to his complicated ablutions, such as might have been practiced by an implicit believer in the method of the Abbé Kneipp*... or by a professional prostitute. He was still swathed in moist linen, over which he wore a sort of monk's robe of coarse wool, a hygienic garment that he called his "Spanish cloak."

It was then that Ellen appeared.

An increasingly acute humming sound had announced her arrival. It sounded like a steamer's siren, and all the

---

*Sebastian Kneipp (1821-97), a Bavarian priest and healer, was the inventor of a method of hydrotherapy.

time it continued Marcueil thought he was hearing the word "siren" in his ears.

A monstrous automobile — the unique racing model recently invented by Arthur Gough and propelled by explosive mixtures the secret of which belonged to William Elson — the same vehicle in which Elson and his daughter had left on the preceding evening, but this time piloted by Ellen alone — had rushed headlong, as fleet as a hippogriff, toward the flight of steps leading to the entrance.

Siren: the name had been suggested to Marcueil by the whirring of the motor, which had made the windowpanes of Lurance vibrate. The pink plush driver's mask Ellen wore gave her head a curiously birdlike appearance, and Marcueil remembered that the real sirens of the fable were not sea monsters, but supernatural sea birds.

She removed her mask with a gesture like a man's salute.

She was a small woman — a little slip of one, as the general had said — dark-haired and pale, save for a little color in her cheeks, round-faced with a slightly snub nose, thin-lipped, with immense eyelashes and practically no eyebrows, so that, seen in profile, her brown lashes seemed to detach themselves from her face, and one could imagine — for her hair was hidden under her leather headgear — that she was a blonde.

After a few banal phrases, Ellen said:

"My visit is not *comme il faut.*"

Marcueil, wrapped in his Spanish cloak, could hardly have been said to be dressed to receive a guest. Yet, however bizarre and outlandish his garb, it was rather in keeping with a certain monastic modesty, containing him in its coarse folds from his neck to his ankles. Ellen unaffectedly allowed her gaze to descend to his bare feet in their wooden sandals, extraordinarily small feet like those of the fauns on antique vases. All she could see was the curve of the heel and the big toe; the arch of his sole was lost in his robe like the rising of some Lilliputian vault.

She murmured, like a password to be understood by Marcueil and herself alone: "The Indian so celebrated by Theophrastus..." Marcueil, who was not wearing his pince-nez, lowered his gaze suddenly, as though to conceal his soul — or any other inner thing — from the girl.

Ellen calmly continued the unreciprocated dialogue:

"Guess why I believe in the 'Indian'? Because no one else will... thank goodness! Besides, in public I won't believe in him... Don't be surprised, when we see each other again in some drawing room, to hear me mock more, and more savagely, than any other woman — this Man whose strength knows no bounds..."

"How many lovers have you had?" asked Marcueil, with cold simplicity.

Without answering this question, she said:

"So you like numbers? All right: there is one chance out of a thousand that the 'Indian' exists, and that one chance justifies my having come. There are a thousand chances to one — and this is important for my reputation — that no one will believe in the Indian's existence. That makes a total, then, of one thousand and one good reasons for my coming to see you."

"How many were they?" repeated Marcueil, with some insolence.

"But... they weren't, my dear sir," said Ellen, with dignity.

"To lie is classically feminine, but vague," said Marcueil.

"They did not count in the eyes of the world, which never knew of them, nor in my own, for I was merely dreaming! The Absolute Lover must exist, since woman can conceive of him, just as there is but one proof of the immortality of the soul, which is that man, through fear of nothingness, aspires to it!"

"Ouch!" said Marcueil to himself, for he did not like scholasticism, nor any other kind of philosophy or literature, perhaps because he knew them too well. Then, aloud, not to be outdone in pedantry, he located the quotation: *"Ipsissima verba sancti Thomas."*

"And so," said Ellen, with great simplicity, "I believe in him because no one else will... *because it is absurd...* as I believe in God! Firstly, because if others believed in him, I should no longer have him all to myself, I should be jealous and deceived; and then I like remaining a virgin in the only way that is both compatible with voluptuousness and recognized by society: one is a virgin when two conditions are fulfilled: that one is unmarried, and that one's lover is unknown... or impossible!"

"The Indian for a lover, you say," repeated Marcueil. "I suppose you must be several women?"

And his voice changed, and took on a paternal mild-
ness, as though he were consoling a child whom he was
depriving of a toy that he thought it imprudent to give her.

"The 'Indian' is either a curiosity or a fiction, he's not
an amusement! It requires a lot of little precautions!
After... *eleven,* for example, to mention only the rudiments,
and since we cannot avoid numbers... just before we come
to the limits of human capacities — the pleasure must be
somewhat akin to what the teeth of a saw must feel when
they're being ground by a file! Compresses and liniments
have to be used."

"After eleven," Ellen noted. "Then what?"

"Then, somewhere far along in the series of numbers,
there comes the point where the woman writhes, howling,
and runs around the room like — the popular expression is
admirable! — like a poisoned rat! Then there is... but then,
perhaps there is no Indian. It's simpler that way."

When a man and a woman talk so calmly for so long,
the chances are that one or the other of them is hoping that
they are not far from falling into each other's arms.

"You're heartless!" cried Ellen.

"I... have no heart, madame, so be it," said Marcueil,
"and so I must substitute something else for it... since you
have come."

He bit his lip and opened the window.

Their conversation ceased to be private as, through the
large French window, it was now within the hearing of the
servants bustling about in the courtyard.

Ellen seized Marcueil's hand.

"Do you read palms?" he inquired mockingly, pretending not to understand the simple gesture.

"No, but I read eyes, your eyes which I see quite naked today, and in which I see that, if there is such a thing as metempsychosis, somewhere in ancient times you were a very, very old courtesan..."

"All courtesans are queens," replied Marcueil, just to say something insignificant, and brushing Ellen's glove with his hairy lips with impassive courtesy.

The glove convulsed, like a small excited or irritated animal. Marcueil would not have been very surprised to hear it bark. At the bottom of the steps, with feverish fingers, Ellen broke the stem of a red rose.

Marcueil, still serious, interpreted this gesture:

"So you're fond of flowers?"

He affected to believe that it was a mere caprice, and to excuse himself for not having anticipated it. The roses of Lurance would have justified it; they were of immemorial fame, with several unique varieties among them. Marcueil opened a pocketknife and went over to the flower bed.

Miss Elson refused with a movement of her head.

"It's not worth it. I'm leaving tomorrow. It's true I should have liked their scent and color to brighten up the long track and the smoky cars for me, but they would die."

With a readiness that shocked her, Marcueil put away his knife.

"I forgot, the big race. Yes... they mustn't die..."

Ellen, not wanting to admit that she found Marcueil's manner a trifle too brutally discourteous, abruptly got back into her car, which snorted.

Bereft of ornaments and comforts, under a simple coat of red-lead paint, the machine exhibited without modesty, almost with pride, its organs of propulsion. It seemed like a lewd and fabulous god carrying off the girl. But, with a sort of crown, she turned the head of the docile monster wherever she willed, to left and to right. The dragons of legend are all crowned.

The metallic beast, like a huge beetle, fluttered its wing-sheaths, scratched the ground, trembled, agitated its feelers, and departed.

Ellen, in her pale-green dress, seemed like a tiny alga clinging to a gigantic coral trunk being carried away by a rushing torrent...

Marcueil, deep in thought, listened to the diminishing hum of the motor. The memory of it sounded in his ears long after the actual sound had disappeared.

"They mustn't die," he thought.

Then, as though awakening from sleep, he called the gardener and ordered him to cut all the roses.

5

THE TEN-THOUSAND-MILE RACE

William Elson was over forty when his daughter Ellen was born. In the year 1920 he was more than a sexagenarian, but the suppleness of his tall frame, the vigor of his health, and the lucidity of his mind belied the years and the whiteness of his beard.

He had won fame by his toxicological discoveries, and had been appointed president of all the new temperance societies in the United States from the day when, by an anticipated reversal of scientific fashion, it was proclaimed that the only hygienic beverage was pure alcohol.

It is to William Elson that we owe the philanthropic invention of denaturing the water piped into homes so as to render it undrinkable, while leaving it fit for toilet purposes.

On his arrival in France, his theories were disputed by several physicians who still clung to the earlier doctrines. His most bitter opponent was Doctor Bathybius.

Dining with Elson in a restaurant one day, the doctor alleged, among other things, that he was certain he could detect an alcoholic tremor in his hand.

Old Elson's only reply was to draw out his revolver and aim it at the push button of the electric bell.

"Merely a quick eye, you might object," said he to the doctor. "Then please hold this menu card in front of my face."

His hand did not move after the screen was interposed. He fired.

The weapon fired dumdum bullets. Nothing was left of the bell push, very little of the wall, and a few intermittent screams were heard from the neighboring compartment where a peaceful patron had been interrupted in the middle of his hors d'oeuvres. But, for a second, the electric push button, struck dead center, had transmitted an impulse to the bell.

The waiter appeared.

"Another bottle of alcohol," Elson ordered.

Such was the man whose work had led him to the discovery of Perpetual Motion Food.

Having at length produced his Perpetual Motion Food, it was not an unprecedented event when William Elson, together with Arthur Gough, decided to launch his product by a great race between a bicycle team, whose only food it was to be, and an express train. In America, from the last few years of the nineteenth century, five- and six-man bicycle teams had many times beaten express trains over one or two miles. What was unheard of, though, was the claim that the human mechanism was superior to the machine *over long distances.* The fine confidence in his discovery that his success afterward inspired in William Elson was

to bring him little by little to share André Marcueil's ideas
on the limitlessness of human strength. Yet, as a practical
man, he could only judge it limitless with the aid of his
Perpetual Motion Food.

As for the question of whether or not André Marcueil
took part in the race, although Miss Elson was convinced
that she had recognized him there, that we leave to be
judged from this chapter. For greater precision, we shall
take our account of this race, known as the Perpetual
Motion Food Race, or the Ten-Thousand-Mile Race, from
one of the members of the five-man bicycle team, Ted
Oxborrow, as reported by and published in the *New York
Herald:*

Lying horizontally on the five-man bicycle — standard
1920 racing model, no handle bars, fifteen-millimeter
tires, development 57.34 meters — our faces lower than
our saddles, sheltered behind masks from wind and dust,
our ten legs joined on either side by aluminum rods, we
started off down the interminable, 10,000-mile-long
track that had been prepared alongside the lines of the great
express. At first we were towed by a bullet-shaped car at the
provisional speed of 120 kilometers per hour.

We were strapped tightly to the machine, so that we
didn't fall off, in this order: at the back, myself — Ted
Oxborrow; in front of me, Jewey Jacobs, George Webb,
Sammy White — a Negro — and Bill Gilbey, the leader of
our team, whom we jokingly called *Corporal* Gilbey because
he was in charge of four men. I don't count a dwarf, Bob
Rumble, tossing in a trailer behind us, whose counter-

weight served to increase or decrease the traction of our rear wheel.

At regular intervals Corporal Gilbey passed to us over his shoulder the small, colorless, crumbly, and bitter-tasting cubes of Perpetual Motion Food that were our only nourishment for nearly five days. He took them five at a time from a small platform behind the starting car. Beneath this platform glowed the white dial of the speedometer, and underneath the dial a revolving drum was suspended, to cushion any shocks to the front wheel of our machine.

When night began to fall, this drum, unseen by the people on the train, was connected to the wheels of the starting car so as to revolve in the opposite direction to them. Corporal Gilbey had us pull forward so that our front wheel rested against the drum; they locked together like gears, and we were towed, effortlessly and fraudulently, during the first hours of the night.

Sheltered behind the starting car, there was of course not a breath of air. On our right the locomotive, looking like a big, good-natured animal, seemed to be grazing in the same part of our visual "field," neither advancing nor receding. Its only apparent motion was a slight trembling of its flank — where, apparently, the drive shaft was oscillating. In front it had a cowcatcher whose bars, which looked like prison bars or the grille on a water mill, could be counted. It was all rather like a peaceful scene by a river — the silent flow of the smooth track being the river itself, and the regular bubbling of the great beast seeming like the sound of a waterfall.

I caught several glimpses of Mr. Elson, with his long white beard, through the windows of the first car, rocking up and down as though nonchalantly seated in a rocking chair.

The big, curious eyes of Miss Elson also appeared for a moment at the first door of the second car, which was as far as I could see by craning my neck.

Mr. Gough's small, busy, blond-mustached silhouette never left the platform of the locomotive. For, although William Elson was following the race aboard the train, it was nevertheless in the hope of seeing the train beaten, while for Mr. Gough, the large sum he had wagered stimulated him to exert every effort of his engine-driving abilities.

Sammy White was humming, in time with the strokes of our legs, the little nursery rhyme:

Twinkle, twinkle, little star...

And, in the solitude of the night, the falsetto voice of Bob Rumble, who was feeble-minded, yelped behind us:

"Something's following us!"

Nothing, either living or mechanical, however, could have followed us at that speed, and besides, the people on the train were able to keep an eye on the level, empty track behind Bob Rumble. It is true that it was impossible to see the last few yards of the track behind the cars, for they only had lateral openings, and we riders could not look behind us. But it would have been most unlikely that anyone could have been traveling on that bumpy track. The dwarf must have been expressing his pride at having his puerile self towed behind us.

When the second day dawned, a strident and snoring sound, an immense vibration in which we seemed to be bathed, nearly drew the blood from my ears. I heard that the last, bullet-shaped car had been "turned loose," and then replaced by a trumpet-shaped flying machine. It was revolving on its own axis, corkscrewing through the air just above the ground in front of us, while a furious wind was sucking us toward its funnel. The silken thread of the speedometer was still quivering regularly, tracing a vertical blue spindle against Corporal Gilbey's cheek, and I read on its ivory dial, as had been predicted for that time, the number of kilometers per hour:

250

The train had retained its previous position, with the same apparent immobility, prodigiously verifiable by all my senses, and even by the touch of my right hand; but the waterfall noise had become hyperacute, and just one millimeter away from the locomotive's incandescent furnace, because of the speed, it was deathly cold.

Mr. W. Elson was invisible. I looked unhindered through one window after another into his car. Something blocked the glance I tried to cast into Miss Elson's car. The first window of the long mahogany compartment, the only one within my line of sight, was obstructed, to my great stupefaction, *on the outside,* by a thick, scarlet covering. It seemed as though a growth of bleeding mushrooms had sprung up on the windowpane overnight...

It was now broad daylight, and I could not doubt what I saw: all that I could glimpse of the car was hidden by red roses; enormous, full-blown, and as fresh as if they had just been picked. Their perfume spread through the stillness of the air behind the shelter of the windshield.

When the girl lowered the window, part of the curtain of flowers was torn, but they did not fall immediately: for several seconds they traveled through space at the same speed as the machines; then the largest one, caught by a sudden gust, was swallowed up inside the car.

It seemed to me that Miss Elson uttered a cry and raised her hand to her breast, and then I saw her no more all that day. The roses gradually shed their petals, owing to the vibration, and flew off, singly or by threes and fours; the varnished wood of the sleeping car reappeared, immaculate, reflecting more clearly than any mirror the ugly profile of Bob Rumble.

The following day the rosy inflorescence was renewed. I wondered whether I was going mad, and Miss Elson's anxious face thenceforth never left the window.

But a more serious incident engaged my attention.

On that morning of the third day a terrible thing occurred; terrible, especially, because it could have cost us the race. Jewey Jacobs, in the seat immediately in front of me, his knees a yard away from my knees, connected by the aluminum rods — Jewey Jacobs, who had been working with fantastic vigor from the very start, so much so that the strength of his pedaling could have thrust our machine forward faster than our schedule permitted, so that I had on several occasions had to pedal against him — Jewey Jacobs suddenly seemed to take a perverse pleasure in straightening his legs in return, pushing my knees up disagreeably against my chin, and forcing me to get down to some serious leg-work.

Neither Corporal Gilbey nor, behind him, Sammy White nor George Webb were able to turn around in their masks and harnesses to see what had got into Jewey Jacobs, but I could bend over sufficiently to catch a glimpse of his right leg; his foot was still thrust into the leather toe-clip and was still moving regularly up and down, but the ankle seemed to have become numb and the ankle-play had ceased. Moreover, and perhaps this is too much of a technicality, I had not taken sufficient notice of a peculiar odor, which I had attributed to his black jersey shorts where, like the rest of us, he satisfied both his needs into some fuller's earth. But a sudden idea made me shudder, and I looked again at the heavy, marble ankle which was within a yard of my leg, and linked to it, and I breathed in the *cadaverous* odor of an incomprehensibly rapid decomposition.

Half a yard off to my right, another sort of change struck me: instead of the middle of the tender, I saw opposite me the second door of the first car.

"We're seizing up!" cried George Webb at that instant.

"We're seizing up!" repeated Sammy White and George Webb; and, as a mental shock weakens the limbs more than physical fatigue, the last door of the second car appeared by my shoulder, the last flowering door of the second and last car. The voices of Arthur Gough and his crew rose in a cheer.

"Jewey Jacobs is dead," I cried, woefully, with all my strength.

The third and second team members roared into their masks, up to Bill Gilbey:

"Jewey Jacobs is dead!"

The sound whirled in the rushing air as far as the sides of the trumpet-shaped flying machine, which repeated three times — for it was enormous enough for two echoes to resound along its length — which repeated from the heights of the heavens onto the fabulous track behind us, like a summons to the Last Judgment:

"Jewey Jacobs is dead! Dead! Dead!"

"Oh! He's dead, is he? I don't give a damn," said Corporal Gilbey. "Stand by: KEEP JACOBS GOING!"

It was a tedious task, such as I hope never to see again in any race. The man was kicking backward, counterpedaling, seizing up. It is extraordinary how this term, which is applied to the friction of machines, was marvelously applicable to the corpse. And it went on doing what it had to do, right under my nose, into its fuller's earth. Ten times we were tempted to unscrew the rods that bound our five pairs of legs together — counting the dead man's. But he was harnessed, padlocked, weighted, packaged, and sealed into his seat — and then... he would have been a... *dead* weight (I can't help the pun) and to win this difficult race we couldn't do with a dead weight.

Corporal Gilbey was a practical man, just as William

Elson and Arthur Gough too were practical gentlemen, and Corporal Gilbey ordered us to do what they themselves would have ordered. Jewey Jacobs was under contract to be fourth man in the great and honorable Perpetual Motion Food Race; he had signed a paper that would have set him back twenty-five thousand dollars for nonperformance, payable on his future races. If he were dead, he could no longer race, and would be unable to pay. So he had to race, then, alive or dead. One can sleep on a bike, so one should be able to die on a bike with no more trouble. And besides, this was called the *perpetual motion* race!

William Elson explained to us later that the stiffness of a corpse, which he called *rigor mortis,* I believe, means absolutely nothing, and can be overcome by the slightest effort. As for the sudden putrefaction, he himself admitted that he did not know its cause. Perhaps, he said, it was due to the secretion of an extraordinary abundance of muscular toxins.

Soon Jewey Jacobs began to pedal, with a bad grace at first, and we couldn't see whether he was making any grimaces, as his face was still in his mask. We encouraged him with friendly insults of the sort that our grandfathers used to shout at Terront, during the first Paris-Brest race: "Get going, you pig!" Little by little he entered into the swing of it, his legs caught up with ours, the ankle-play returned, and finally he started pedaling madly.

"He's acting as a flywheel," said the corporal. "He's steadying, and I think he's about to race."

Indeed, not only did he catch up with us, he increased his speed beyond ours, and Jacobs' death-sprint was a

sprint the like of which the living cannot conceive. So much
so that the last car, which had disappeared during the time
it took us to train the deceased, grew larger and larger, and
resumed its normal place, which it never should have left,
with the middle of the tender half a yard off my right
shoulder. All this did not take place, naturally enough,
without our cheers being raised, thundered into our four
masks:

"Hip, hip, hurray for Jewey Jacobs!"

And the flying trumpet echoed throughout the skies:

"Hip, hip, hurray for Jewey Jacobs!"

I had lost sight of the locomotive and its two cars while
we were teaching the dead to live; when he was able to get
along by himself I saw the rear of the last car growing big-
ger as though it were coming back to hear the latest news. It
was no doubt a hallucination — the distorted reflection of
the five-man machine in the mahogany of the great sleeping car, more limpid than a mirror — but I saw what looked
like a hunchbacked human being — hunchbacked or bearing some enormous burden — pedaling along behind the
train. His legs were moving at exactly the same speed as
ours.

Instantly, the vision disappeared, hidden by the back
corner of the car, which we had already passed. I thought it
very comical to hear the ridiculous Bob Rumble, panic-
stricken and jumping from side to side of his wicker seat
like a monkey in a cage, yapping as before:

"There's something pedaling, there's something following us!"

The education of Jewey Jacobs had taken us a whole

day. It was the morning of the fourth day, three minutes, seven and two-fifths seconds after nine o'clock, and the speedometer was at its farthest limit, which it had not been designed to exceed: 300 kilometers per hour.

The flying machine was of great help to us, and though I don't know whether we exceeded the previously recorded speed, I am sure that it was responsible for our not slowing down, as the needle of the speedometer remained at the far end of the dial. The train kept up with us steadily, but they could not have foreseen such high speeds when taking on fuel, for the passengers — there were no others than Mr. Elson and his daughter — passed through the corridor to the platform of the locomotive, near the engine driver, bringing their food and drink with them. The girl seemed marvelously active, and was carrying a dressing case. They were all busy — there were five or six in all — breaking up the cars and throwing everything combustible into the fire-box.

Our speed increased, I cannot tell how much, but the hum of the flying machine rose several semitones, and it felt as though the resistance to the pedals had completely ceased — which was absurd, seeing that my efforts were redoubled. Could it be that the amazing Jewey Jacobs had made even further progress?

Now I no longer saw the unvarying asphalt track beneath my feet, but — very far away — the top of the loco-motive! The smoke from the coal and kerosene blinded us in our masks. The flying machine seemed to be creeping along.

"Vulture's glide," explained Corporal Gilbey curtly, between fits of coughing. "Watch out for the fall!"

It is known, as Arthur Gough could explain better than I, that a body in motion, moving at a high speed, rises in a glide, its speed overcoming its adherence to the ground. It will, of course, fall back again, if it is not provided with some organs designed to propel it through space.

Our five-man cycle, when it fell, vibrated like a tuning fork.

"All right," said the corporal suddenly, with an odd gesture, his nose up against his front wheel. We were now again moving as before.

"Front tire blown," said Bill in reassuring tones.

On our right there was no longer any trace of the cars. Enormous piles of wood and cans of gasoline were heaped on the tender. The cars had been detached and left behind; even if their momentum had allowed them to follow for a time, their vibration would have sufficed to hold them back. It was now possible to follow the movement of the wheels. The locomotive was still at the same level. "Vulture's glide again," said Bill Gilbey. "Can't fall now. Rear tire blown. All right."

I was so astonished that I raised my head over the top of my horizontal mask and looked into the air. The flying machine had disappeared and had doubtless been left behind somewhere with the abandoned cars.

Everything was going well, however, as the corporal had said; the speedometer, trembling against his cheek, was still marking a regularly increasing top speed, which had long since been in excess of three hundred kilometers per hour.

The turning point could now be seen on the horizon.

It was a great tower, open to the sky, shaped like a truncated cone, two hundred yards in diameter at the base and a hundred yards high. Massive stone and iron buttresses supported it. The race track and the rails were swallowed up in it through a sort of gateway and, inside, for a fraction of a minute, we whirled lying over on our sides, and held by our momentum to the walls, which were not only vertical but overhanging, like the underside of a roof. We seemed like flies racing along on a ceiling.

The locomotive was suspended on its side beneath us, like a shelf on a wall. A thrumming sound filled the truncated cone.

And then, in that fraction of a minute, in the middle of this isolated tower on the trans-Siberian steppe, as we emerged from its empty interior, we all heard the echo of a loud voice that seemed to have entered immediately behind the locomotive. This voice cursed, swore, and fulminated.

I distinctly made out this preposterous phrase, uttered in good English — doubtless so that it should not be lost on us:

"You're cutting my shoulder, you hog's head!"

Then a muffled impact.

We were already coming out of the curve, and, through the sort of gateway we had a few seconds before found empty, we now came upon a barrel of that very capacity that the English call a *hogshead*, holding fifty-four gallons — with a large rectangular opening at its bung and, near the middle, provided with two straps like the shoulder straps of a soldier's knapsack, as though it had been carried on a man's back. This barrel was rocking, like any rounded object that has just been brutally flung down on the ground, like a child's cradle.

The cowcatcher of the locomotive hit it like a football, spattering the rails and the track with a little water and sheaves of roses. Some of them, still revolving, stuck on to our blown-out tires by their thorns.

The night of the fourth day was falling. Although it had taken us three days to reach the turn, if we continued at the same speed we should be at the finish of the Ten Thousand Miles within twenty-four hours.

As the darkness came on I cast one last glance at the speedometer, which I would not be seeing again before the dawn. As I looked, the silken thread, writhing and trembling at the edge of the speedometer frame, flared up in the form of a bright blue spindle, and suddenly all was dark.

Then, as though under a shower of meteorites, blows rained down upon us, blows both hard and soft, sharp, feathery, bleeding, howling, and lugubrious, caught in our speeding path like flies, and our machine swerved and bumped against the still seemingly motionless locomotive. They remained in contact for the space of a few yards, though the mechanical movements of our legs did not stop.

"Nothing," said the corporal. "Birds."

We were no longer sheltered behind the tow cars, and it is remarkable that no such accident had befallen us earlier, as soon as the flying funnel was released.

At that moment, without even a word from the corporal, the midget, Bob Rumble, crawled toward me on his tow rod, to bring all his weight to bear on the rear wheel and so increase its traction. This maneuver informed me that our speed was still increasing.

I heard the chatter of his teeth, and realized that Bob Rumble had only come closer to escape what he called the "something following us."

Behind my back, and a little to the left, he lit an acetylene lamp which oddly cast, in front of us and somewhat to our right (the locomotive now being on our left), the fivefold shadow of our team on the white track.

In the cheerful light, the dwarf was no longer complaining. And we kept pace WITH OUR SHADOW.

I no longer had any idea how fast we were going. I tried to catch a few snatches of the silly little songs Sammy White was humming to himself to keep his pedaling in time. Just before the speedometer needle had gone up in flames he had been jabbering the refrain, like a burst of hail, of his final sprint, so well known from his record-breaking mile and half-mile races on the hairpin tracks of Massachusetts:

Poor Papa paid Peter's potatoes!*

Beyond that he would have had to improvise, but his legs were going too quickly for his brain.

Thought, at least Sammy White's, is not so rapid as they say, and I can't see it going on exhibition on any track.

There is really only one record that it will be a long

---

* In English in the original.

time before either Sammy White, the world champion, or I, or our five-man team, will beat; the record of light, and I have seen it beaten with my own eyes. When the lamp was lit behind us, sweeping our shadow forward along the track, the five members of our shadow were grouped for an instant so as to seem, fifty yards in front of us, like a single racer seen from behind, riding in front of us. Our simultaneous pedal strokes completed the illusion — which I heard afterwards was not an illusion. When our shadow was thrown forward we all felt sharply and distinctly that some silent and unbeatable opponent, who must have been watching us for days, had taken off on our right at the same time as our shadow, hidden within it, and kept fifty yards ahead. So well did we emulate it that the rods linking our legs began to oscillate with no less force than that with which a mad dog turns on its own tail, for want of something better to bite.

Yet the locomotive, burning its cars, was still at the same level, giving the impression of a great calm near a geyser... It seemed to carry no living soul besides Miss Elson, who was following with an overexcited and inexplicable curiosity the contortions — which were certainly fairly grotesque — of our distant shadow. William Elson, Arthur Gough, and the mechanics stood motionless. As for ourselves, lined up in the pale light of our lamp, and so cramped into our masks that we were only slightly caressed by the mighty hurricane created by our speed, we were reliving, I think, to judge from my own feelings, our evenings as children, under the lamplight, bending over our homework on the table. And we seemed to be re-creating one of my visions on such an evening: a large death's-head moth had gotten in my window and, taking no notice, curiously enough, of the lamp, went seeking with warlike passion its own shadow cast on the ceiling by the flame, banging it again and again with all the battering rams of its hairy body: whack, whack, whack...

Immersed in these thoughts or this reverie, I did not notice that the vibrations caused by our speed had put out the lamp, and yet the same odd outline, still visible because the track was very white and the night quite clear, was "leading the pack" fifty yards in front!

It could not have been projected by the locomotive's headlamps: the very kerosene from both lamps had long since gone to add more heat to the darkening boiler.

Still, there is no such thing as a ghost — then what could this *shadow* be?

Corporal Gilbey hadn't noticed that our lamp had gone out, otherwise he would have sharply reprimanded Bob Rumble. Jovial and practical as ever, he encouraged us with his catcalls:

"Come on, boys, let's catch up with it! It can't hold out for long! We're gaining on it. It's running out of oil; that's no shadow, it's a turnspit!"

In the vast silence of the night, we hurried even more.

Suddenly... I heard... I thought I heard something like the chirping of a bird, but it had a singularly metallic tone.

I was not mistaken: there was a noise, somewhere in front, a clanking noise...

I was sure of what was causing it, and I wanted to cry

out, to call the corporal, but I was too terrified by my discovery.

The shadow was creaking like an old weathercock!

There was no longer any doubt about the only really extraordinary occurrence of the race: the appearance of the ROAD HOG.

And yet I shall never believe that anyone, man or devil, could have followed — and passed — us during the Ten Thousand Miles!

Especially considering the way he was gotten up! This is what must have happened: the Road Hog, who had let us catch up with him, naturally, and was keeping to the left, almost in front of the locomotive; the Road Hog, coming up at the very instant when the shadow disappeared, and merging for a second with it, crossed the track in front of our machine with incredible awkwardness but with providential luck, both for him and for us. On his apocalyptic machine, he went veering into the first rail... You would have thought, my goodness, from the amount of zigzagging he was doing, that he hadn't ridden a bicycle for more than three hours in his life. He crossed the first rail at right angles, at the risk of his life, and he looked quite desperate, as if he knew he would never cross the second. Hypnotized by the functioning of his handlebars, his eyes on his front wheel, he did not appear to realize that he was carrying out his imbecilic little maneuvers in front of a great express train that was booming down on him at more than three hundred kilometers an hour. He seemed suddenly struck with some extremely prudent and ingenious idea, swerved sharply to the right, and took off down the gravel straight in front of him, fleeing before the locomotive. At precisely that instant the front of the machine caught up with his rear wheel.

During that second when he was about to be crushed to pulp, everything about his comical silhouette, down to the details of the spokes in his bicycle wheels, remained photographically imprinted on my retinas. Then I closed my eyes, not wishing to count his ten thousand fragments.

He wore pince-nez, was practically clean-shaven, and had just a small, sparse, curly beard.

He was dressed in a frock coat and wore a top hat gray with dust. His right trouser leg was rolled up as if for the express purpose of being more likely to get entangled in his chain, and his left leg was caught up in a lobster-claw clip. His feet, on their rubber pedals, were in elastic-sided boots. His machine was a straight-framed, balloon-tired model of a type now worth its weight in gold — and it must have been heavy! — what with iron mudguards fore and aft. Many of its spokes — direct spokes — had been industriously replaced by whalebone umbrella stays whose forks, which had not been removed, whirled around in the shape of a figure eight.

Surprised to hear the regular clicking, as well as the grating sound of the worn bearings, a good half-minute after what I had supposed must be the catastrophe, I opened my eyes again and couldn't believe them — I couldn't even believe that they were open. The Road Hog was still gliding along on our left, on the track! The locomotive was up against him and he seemed in no way inconvenienced by it. Then I saw the explanation of this marvel: the wretched fellow was no doubt unaware of the arrival of the great train behind him otherwise he would not have shown such perfect composure. The locomotive had bumped into his bicycle and was now pushing it *by the rear mudguard!* As for the chain — for of course the ridiculous and senseless character would not have been able to move his legs at such a speed — the chain had been snapped in two by the impact, and the Road Hog was pedaling joyfully in space — needlessly, moreover, since the elimination of all transmission constituted for him an excellent and uncontrolled "free wheeling" — congratulating himself on his performance which he attributed, no doubt, to his natural capacities!

The light of an apotheosis appeared on the horizon, and the Road Hog was the first to appear in its aureole. It was the illumination of the terminal point of the Ten Thousand Miles!

I had the impression that a nightmare was ending.

"Come on! One more effort," the corporal was saying. "The five of us should be able to leave our buddy behind!"

This clear voice — in the same way as the sight of a fixed landmark emphasizes the rolling of a ship to a seasick man lying in his hammock — that voice of the corporal made me realize that I was drunk, dead drunk from fatigue or from the alcohol in our Perpetual Motion Food — Jewey Jacobs had died of it, hadn't he? — and sobered me at the same time.

Nevertheless, I had not dreamed: a strange runner was in front of the locomotive, but he was not riding a straight-framed, balloon-tired machine! But he was not wearing elastic-sided boots! But his bicycle was not creaking, except in my buzzing eardrums! But he had not broken his chain, since his bicycle was a machine without a chain! The ends of a loose, black strap floated behind him and caressed the front of the locomotive! This was what I had taken for a mudguard, and for the tails of a frock coat! The swelling of his extensor muscles had torn his shorts over his thighs! His bicycle was a racing model the like of which I had never seen, with microscopic tires and a development greater than that of our machine; he was pedaling with the greatest of ease and, indeed, as if his pedals were disconnected. The man was in front of us: I saw the back of his neck, wild with long hair; the cord of his pince-nez — or a black lock of hair — was pushed right back onto his shoulders by the breeze caused by the race. The muscles of his calves were palpitating like two alabaster hearts.

There was a movement on the platform of the loco-motive, as though some momentous event were about to take place. Arthur Gough gently pushed back Miss Elson, who was leaning forward to watch, with love, it seemed, the unknown racer. The engineer seemed to be conferring with Mr. Elson in sharp tones, apparently trying to exact some exorbitant concession from him. The old man's beseeching voice reached me:

"You're not going to give it to the locomotive to drink? It would hurt it! It's not a human creature! You're not going to kill this animal!"

After a few rapid and unintelligible phrases:

"Then let me make the sacrifice myself! Let me only be separated from it at the last instant!"

The white-bearded chemist raised a phial in his hands with infinite precaution. It contained, I have since learned, an admirable rum that could have been his ancestor, and that he had been saving to drink alone; he poured this ultimate fuel into the locomotive's boiler... The alcohol was no doubt too admirable: the machine went psshhhh... and went out.

So it was that the Perpetual Motion Food's five-man cycle won the Ten-Thousand-Mile Race; but neither Corporal Gilbey nor Sammy White nor George Webb nor Bob Rumble nor, I think, Jewey Jacobs in the other world nor I, Ted Oxborrow, who sign this report for all of them, will ever be able to console ourselves for finding, when we arrived at the finish post — where no one was waiting for us, since no one had foreseen so prompt an arrival — this post crowned with red roses, the same haunting red roses that had blazed the trail during the entire race...

No one has been able to tell us what became of the fantastic racer.

6

THE ALIBI

The same morning, back at Lurance, Marcueil had several pneumatic letters taken to a Paris post office.

To Doctor Bathybius he wrote:

My dear Doctor,

Don't be annoyed with me any more because of my paradoxes: the Indian has been found. No scientist is more worthy than you to be his Theophrastus, nor to occupy what you termed the other day "a chair in the department of the impossible."

Do come tonight.

A. M.

To the seven most highly quoted tarts on the day's love exchange, he sent the address of the Château de Lurance and the time of the reception, scrawled in black with the edge of a silver coin across a bank note — although it is forbidden to send valuables in a *pneumatique.*

To his intimates, but "for men only," as it says on carnival posters — and only to those intimates who were bachelors or widowers — he sent a brief invitation, engraved on a visiting card. William Elson was not informed for, although his daughter went out without him, he seldom went out without his daughter. In any case, it was to be presumed that he was recuperating from the fatigue of his journey.

The courtesans were the first to arrive.

The general next.

Then Bathybius.

"What sort of joke is this?" were the doctor's first words.

Paying no attention to his nods of doubt and annoyance, Marcueil explained what he wanted of him. It was simply a matter — "Simply!" cried Bathybius — of supervising an attempt by an "Indian," in the great hall of Lurance, between midnight and midnight, to beat the record "so celebrated by Theophrastus." The great hall, where a large divan-bed had been prepared for the occasion, had been selected not for its size but because a small adjoining room took its light from it by means of a small bull's-eye window, which allowed everything that happened in the hall to be seen. In this retreat, now converted into a washroom, Bathybius could also carry out any examinations he might deem necessary to determine the authenticity of the experiment.

Bathybius was perplexed.

"Where is the Indian?" he finally inquired.

The women were already there, said Marcueil, but the Indian would not arrive until suppertime. Also, supper would be early, at eleven.

After a short hesitation the doctor agreed to undertake the singular role Marcueil was asking him to play. Actually, all that was required was that he enjoy the pleasant hospitality of Lurance for twenty-four hours. As for the problematical "Indian" and his "record," in his glassed-off retreat he would have a front seat from which to laugh at his failure — and also a front seat from which to observe for twenty-four hours the seven prettiest harlots in Paris, without a great deal of covering and in most intriguing attitudes. Now the doctor was an elderly man.

The general's entry was blustery and cordial, as usual.

"What's become of you, my young friend, and what are you doing that's new? Have you stopped wrecking urinals?"

Marcueil did not understand to begin with, but then he remembered.

"What urinals? But, my dear general, you can't call it wrecking a device, just demonstrating that it isn't strong enough to withstand the use it is designed for!"

"He, he!" laughed the general, as Bathybius briefly outlined the attraction for the evening. "Let's hope the little women will be strong enough."

"There are seven of them," said Marcueil.

Whereupon the general bustled off in the direction of the drawing room.

It was ten o'clock, and André Marcueil was looking for an excuse to slip off *to make way for the Indian.* Chance — or perhaps some previously determined assistance brought about by chance — supplied him with one.

"Someone," said a valet, "wishes to speak to monsieur."

This "someone," when he was then ushered into the study, proved to be a policeman.

Not one of those horrific, mustachioed policemen whom we were inured to in our childhood by Punch and Judy shows, but a beardless policeman in undress uniform — so un-dress, in fact, that you would have thought he was hardly even a postman — rolling between his fingers a mere *képi* instead of the legendary three-cornered hat.

The honest lad seemed much embarrassed by the delicacy of his mission.

"Speak up, my good fellow," said Marcueil good-naturedly, and to help him appreciate this good nature he rang for a drink.

The policeman tasted the rum, and praised it with much the same obsequiousness as he might have employed were he glorifying the man who was giving it to him. He obviously wanted to obtain Marcueil's favor.

He began:

"The Service being what it is... the Service... well, we happened to run across — not on purpose, of course! — but we ran across a little girl who had been raped, and who'd been dead six days, here in the Lurance grounds; she'd died from very irregular causes. She hadn't been raped first and killed afterward, the way it usually happens, but — how shall I say it? — *raped to death.*"

He expressed himself hesitantly, but quite correctly, and with a sparing use of adjectives.

"Six days ago?" asked Marcueil. "Justice is slow... six days ago... The day I left, as a matter of fact; I've been away

on a little trip... with some friends... on a train. They were
on the train... A strange excursion! There were some other
rapes, by a curious coincidence, and an armed robbery,
too, as if by chance, and, no one knows how, two murders.
But you were saying: a rape on the Lurance grounds?"

He frowned and rang again.

"Send in Mathieu, the gamekeeper."

Scarcely had the guard arrived when:

"Excuse me, monsieur," broke in the policeman,
before the gamekeeper had had a chance to say anything.
"Actually there were some rifle traps that went off, and it
was the justice of the peace who discovered the little body
when he was on his way to inspect the place... when suddenly, bang! bang! Two shots were fired, and one of them
seriously wounded the poor man in the leg!"

"Mathieu, I was mistaken," said Marcueil. "Neither
your vigilance nor that of your comrades was at fault. You
will receive a reward... You may go."

"You see, constable," he added, "my lands are well
enough guarded for me to have the right to be astonished
to hear that a crime has been discovered on them! Just how
do the French police spend their time?"

"Excuse me, monsieur," said the policeman, "we have
eight villages to look after, and there are only five of us."

"I am not accusing you, my good fellow," condescended Marcueil, liberally refilling his glass with rum.

"The Service is a hard job," continued the policeman.
"Ah! If I'd only known! Before I took to this uniform I was
like your Mr. Mathieu, a gamekeeper over by La Celle-

Saint-Cloud. There was game, in those parts! If you would like to go on a heron shoot around there, in the marshes..."

"I hardly have the leisure, except out of season," said Marcueil, "and I have never troubled to get a shooting license."

The policeman drank, smacked his lips, and winked.

"The season, and the license too, that's up to us!" And he slapped his gaiters. "Excuse me again for bothering you about that little slut — but the Service, you understand!"

"I understand so well," replied Marcueil, "that I have had a special staircase built in honor of such matters."

And, motioning to the wide-eyed policeman to rise, he shone the light from his revolving desk lamp upon a sign above a door, which bore the following legend in beautiful gilded letters:

SERVICE STAIRCASE

The policeman was embarrassed, and looked about him for a place to wipe his boots before leaving.

"Don't thank me," said Marcueil, "it's not you I'm honoring, but your uniform. When next you come to visit me, pray don't come in at the wrong door. The one that leads to this staircase is in the courtyard, and bears a similar inscription. But don't leave like that; the roads are unsafe, according to what you have just told me. You will be driven back to your station in a car."

And Marcueil returned to the drawing room.

He got back just in time to deal with the seven women.

The general had told them of the strange collaboration that was being asked of them and they were angry, and threatening to leave. Marcueil's cold propriety rooted them to the spot, and a second distribution of bank notes restored their grace and their smiles. In a few brief words Marcueil announced that he had some urgent business to transact that would call him away from his guests for a few hours, at any rate during their supper, but that it didn't matter and they were to make themselves at home.

The general asked for a more detailed explanation, but Marcueil's steps were already receding in the hall. Bathybius was suspicious, without knowing why, and slipped out onto the steps. Marcueil was no longer there, but the doctor saw the car leave and heard it moving; he did not discover that, sitting in it, glorious, important, and alone, was the policeman.

Ten minutes later, eleven o'clock struck.

The butler opened the doors of the supper room.

The "Indian" had not yet appeared.

The seven women, taking the men's arms, went in.

There was a slim redhead, with hair like copper, there were four brunettes, with either pale or golden complexions, and there were two blondes, one a little one, her ash-colored hair parted in the middle, the other a fat one, dimpled all over, and with an enamel complexion.

They answered to the modest Christian names — which were perhaps not their own, but they answered to them nonetheless! — of Adèle, Blanche, Eupure, Herminie, Irène, Modeste, and Virginie, which were followed by surnames too whimsical for it to be necessary to mention.

Three had come in high-necked dresses, the most her-
metic that could be imagined, but which could be undone
by a single clasp, and they were all naked underneath. Four,
following the fashion of the day, were wearing fur-lined
driving coats, and when they were taken off for them in the
lobby the women appeared to be lace-embroidered rather
than dressed; Herminie, in a tone calculated to overexcite
the old men, called her diaphanous covering her *undercoat*.

Suddenly a rapid step, both languid and light, was
heard in the corridor.

"It's Marcueil," said Bathybius. "He must have for-
gotten something, or decided not to go after all."

"He's come back in time," said the general. "We're still
only 'attacking.'"

The door opened and the "Indian" appeared.

Although they had been expecting him, there was an
astonished silence.

The man who came in was a handsome athlete, of average height but of incomparable proportions. He was
hairless — or else very closely shaved or epilated, and he had
a short, forked chin. His black hair, thick and sleek, was
plastered back over his head. His chest was bare, and
revealed a mark under the left breast, and his skin was a
reddish-copper color, but lusterless, as if it had been powdered. He was draped in a whole, gray bearskin, fastened
on one shoulder and at his waist, and its enormous head
hung down on his knees. A pipe and a tomahawk were stuck
in this crude shoulder belt. He wore long leather gaiters,
and moccasins of supple yellow leather, trimmed with por-
cupine quills. He happened to raise one arm, and the

onlookers could distinguish, tattooed in blue on his pumice-stoned armpit, the totem of the llama.

They noticed that the muscles of his armpits and thighs were convex, not concave, a structure that hadn't been seen since the famous weight lifter, Thomas Topham.

"What a handsome creature!" the women cried spontaneously.

They were not, of course, referring to the rudely drawn llama, but to the man.

One is always a handsome creature, for such women, when one shows a little bare flesh.

The Indian said not a word, sat down at the table without looking at them and, like a normal person, or even four, ate.

7

LADIES ONLY

Shortly before midnight a peculiar shyness seized the women, possibly because of the men's allusions, though these were comparatively discreet, and they grew increasingly sensitive to them as the time to justify them drew near. Particularly irritated by the "Mohican" impassiveness of the Indian, the girls slipped off and wandered aimlessly through the winding castle. They went up a staircase and found themselves by chance in a spacious portrait gallery, just off the hall which had been set aside for the "record." It had communicated with the hall in former times, when that vast room had been used for staging entertainments. Imagine an immense box in the first balcony of a theater, but with its view of the stage walled up.

They almost felt as if they were at home there, as they were alone.

Like parakeets when there is no one near their cage, they began a crystalline chatter, deliciously out of tune, like the sound of love instruments tuning up, one might imagine. Downstairs the violins were likewise warming up.

It goes without saying that they spoke of everything except what was on all their minds: the Indian.

"My dears," Blanche was saying, "the most marvelous thing they have invented is to bring back the styles of twenty years ago, the system of corsets with four straps, two in front and two on the sides."

"The ones in front are a waste of space... and time," observe Irène.

"It doesn't matter to me," replied Blanche, "I've a right to say it's wonderful because... I don't wear one myself."

And she pulled up her skirt to exhibit her black socks with pink stitching; pulling it, indeed, much higher than was necessary.

"So you wear socks," said Modeste. "The... savage, I don't know what he's wearing, it looks like a sewerman's boots with spikes."

"Here we go," said Blanche. "I wasn't thinking about him, but joking apart, he's a terribly good-looking man."

"I find him too painted up," said Virginie. "He needs to be sent to the laundry."

"What a well-developed sense of cleanliness she has!" said Herminie. "You'll have your chance, dear madam, to remove his pigments in a little while."

"You don't send Negroes to the laundry," said Eupure, going one better.

"What do you mean, in a little while? After you," said Virginie, "and if there's anything left! According to what the general told me, we'll be 'put through' in alphabetical order."

"If there's anything left of what?" said Adèle. "His paint?"

"I go second," stated Blanche, "but perhaps even that will be a sinecure."

"The idea's a perfect scream, but it will never work," said Irène.

"Let's congratulate the first 'bride,'" said all six, making deep curtsies to Adèle.

There was a rustling sound on the landing.

"Sssh, someone's coming upstairs," murmured Adèle.

"It must be he," said Virginie. "It's a good thing he's thawing out, he only opened his mouth to eat."

"He has nice teeth, he probably only chews broken glass as a rule," said Herminie.

"Ground glass, if he does what they say," corrected Irène.

"Ssh!" said Adèle again.

The same light and rapid step that had announced the Indian's coming, even lighter and more rapid this time, drew near. Something like a nudity or a silken garment brushed against the door.

"His bearskin sounds like a dress," said Blanche.

"They drape themselves like women, in his country..."

"But more décolleté," whispered some voices.

Someone fumbled with the lock. The women were silent.

The door did not open. The footsteps went downstairs again. A clicking of heels was heard, and a burst of laughter, strangely silvery, grew fainter.

"What's it mean?" asked one of the women. "He's not

very polite, that savage."

"He's shy... Hey, Joe! You're forgetting your bearskin!"

"He doesn't know how to behave," explained Virginie, who prided herself on her upbringing.

"Still, he paid up like an African king," said another, "or else his keeper paid up for him."

"How horrible!" said several. "But it's true, he was nice."

"Perhaps he was coming to call us: it'll soon be midnight. Shall we go downstairs, ladies?"

"Yes, let's!" they all said, taking up their hats which they had thrown onto the furniture.

"Come and help me, Virginie," said Adèle. "This door is stuck..."

One by one they tried to open it, then they all pushed together...

Absurd though it seemed, they were locked in!

"It's idiotic," said Virginie. "That savage who doesn't even know French can't ever have seen a lock: he turned it the wrong way. He must have thought he was opening it for us."

"We must call," said Modeste.

Several, not yet frightened, voices, called out:

"Yoo-hoo! Monsieur! Savage! Iroquois! Darling!"

Midnight struck. The clock must have been immediately above the gallery, for its booming filled the long room, the chandelier swayed, the picture frames trembled, and, near the ceiling, a pane of glass vibrated.

"They'll be coming to fetch us," said Adèle. "Let's wait."

"You're in a hurry, being the first; the rest of us have plenty of time," said Blanche.

In a period of waiting interspersed with minor attacks of nerves, they heard a quarter past strike, then half past, a quarter to, and one o'clock.

"What can they be doing down there?" said Modeste. "They must have heard us, though. We can hear the music perfectly well!"

And sure enough, at irregular intervals, the highest notes of the top strings rose like spires piercing through a fog.

They called out again and again, until their faces grew red and they burst into tears.

"Let's do something to pass the time," said Adèle, who wanted to appear calm, and was walking to and fro in front of the portraits. "Ladies, here we are at the Louvre; this tall gentleman with the white wig and the big sword represents..."

"Who?" asked Irène.

"I don't know any more!" And Adèle wept.

The portraits all had the benevolent look of old gentlemen who have just been putting little girls in the corner. *They* didn't seem particularly anxious to leave. At their age people are no longer in a hurry.

One girl threw herself against the high, ironbound door and drummed on it.

As though set off by the beating of her little fists, the

four quarters chimed out, and then the hour — two o'clock.

"Hell!" said Virginie. "I'm going to sleep!"

She stretched herself out on a gilded console, her feet sticking out over the end, her elbows behind her head, and her breasts in the air.

Blanche looked at her from a distance, seated on the round-topped chest, her hands slyly occupied beneath her skirt, her legs dangling.

"Ladies," said Blanche, and she hesitated... "It seems to me that they are doing without us. Perhaps *he* needs some others... perhaps *they* have already begun!"

"Shut up you baby," called out big Irène, erect and furious. She herself did not know how it came about that, wanting to silence her, she closed her mouth with her own.

Modeste, after having paced, sobbing, through the entire gallery, went to hide her desolate face on Virginie's breast. When she stood up again, a humid circle remained on the now transparent blouse, revealing a pink spot — a circle that hadn't been imprinted by her tears.

"It's too hot," said Irène, and some lace flew. "Don't let any men come in now, I'm in my shift."

"All you have to do is take it off," said Eupure.

And Eupure's hand took her by the back of the neck.

Thus it was that, little by little, sobs became sighs, and mouths tormented other realities than tear-filled handker-chiefs. The angry, tapping feet on the carpet were quiet, because the feet were now bare.

Since there was no way out, Virginie shamelessly improvised a murmuring spring on the dyed wool, in a corner.

It was only later, a little before three o'clock, that the electric light disappeared. It was as if the old folk in the portraits had noiselessly gone away... but the groping hands could still find no door!

Seeking a way out, they came up against the derision of a mouth, or genitals.

Then the blue dawn broke and scattered in shivers over the moist bodies.

After which, through a pane high up near the ceiling, the sun swept over the soiled carpet.

It was noon, and the sound of bells, which had inaugurated their imprisonment, was repeated.

The girls were hungry and thirsty, and fought.

One ate her lipstick, and another concocted a perfumed, salted, raw, and execrable loaf out of tears, saliva, and powder.

It was one o'clock, it was any time, then it was eleven o'clock in the evening, and the distant music struck through the silence as confusedly as nervous fingers straining after the eye of the needle.

The electricity still hadn't come on again...

But a light, not daylight, coming from the side, spread through a pane of frosted glass very high up.

The women screamed, rejoiced, kissed each other, bit each other, piled up tables and clambered on them, fell off two or three times, and at last a fist, cuirassed with rings but which bled nevertheless, smashed in the pane.

The women, naked, disheveled, without make-up, famished, in heat, and dirty, threw themselves against the little window open on the light... and on love.

For the iron framework, impassable but allowing them to see, was the only separation between the gallery and the "Indian's" hall.

Although the second midnight had passed, it seemed quite natural to them — they had been thinking about it for so many, and such long, hours — that they should find him there.

The red man's only garment was a naked woman prostrated across his chest; her only covering was a black plush mask.

8

THE OVUM

Twenty-four hours before, Bathybius was going up to the bull's-eye window.

The round pane was covered on the washroom side — the doctor's observatory — by two solid wooden shutters closed by a bolt.

He groped forward and firmly turned the handle with the professional precision he would have employed in turning the endless screw of a speculum.

The shutters parted noiselessly, in the same way as butterflies' wings open.

The window glowed with the golden fire of all the lamps in the hall, and seemed like a star new-risen on the limited horizon of the doctor's table.

In this light Bathybius' eyelids fluttered slightly; his eyes were vague, or rather perpetually fixed upon some invisible point, and their expression was that which, by some unexplained coincidence, is common to most great physicians and a few dangerous monomaniacs living in perpetual confinement. With his handsome, fleshy surgeon's hands, one of which was laden with heavy signet rings, he smoothed apart his flowing white sideburns. He put a sheet of paper on the table, ready for his notes, took out his fountain pen, consulted his watch, and settled down to wait.

Although Bathybius knew perfectly well, being of a grave and thoughtful nature, that he was merely about to observe, on the other side of his round window, some human beings in the most normally and miserably human of attitudes, he advanced toward the window as he would have approached the eyepiece of some prodigious telescope borne up beneath its quivering cupola by colossal wheels and gears, and directed at an unexplored world.

"Now, now," he muttered to himself, "let's not get carried away."

And to drive the vision from his mind, and at the same time see his writing table more clearly, he plugged in a small, turquoise-shaded lamp.

The next night he was most astonished to find, among his papers, and freshly written in his own hand, the strange, scientifico-lyrico-philosophical elucubration that follows. It would seem that he wrote it during his long periods of idleness — that lengthy hour during which the lovers were eating so voraciously, and the ten consecutive hours during which they were sleeping. It is also not impossible that his personality underwent a singular bifurcation, and that one side of him was timing, supervising, analyzing, recording, and checking technical details at every visit of the Indian to the washroom, and the other side of him was generalizing and transforming his impressions into this literary form, which was most unusual for him:

GOD IS INFINITELY SMALL

Who maintains this? Surely not a man.

For man created God, the God he believes in, at any rate, he created him, and it was not God who created man (this is common knowledge today); man created God in his own image and likeness, enlarged to a degree where the human mind can no longer conceive of dimensions.

This does not mean that the God that man conceived is devoid of dimensions.

He is greater than all dimensions, without being beyond dimension; neither immaterial nor infinite. He is only indefinite.

This concept might have sufficed, just before the time when the two people whom we call Adam and Eve were tempted by the manufactured products of the merchants whose totem was the Serpent, and who had to work to acquire them.

We know now that there is another God who did really create man, who resides in the living center of every man, and who is man's immortal soul.

THEOREM: *God is infinitely small.*

Because, for him to be God, his Creation must be infinitely great. Should he retain any dimension, it would be a limitation on his Creation, he would no longer be He who created All.

Thus He may glory in His Goodness, His Loving-kindness, and His Omnipotence, which have no share in the world. God is beyond all dimensions, *but within.*

He is a point.

Q.E.D.

We know that there are two parts in man, one apparent and perishable, the sum of the organs we call the *body,* the *soma,* which perishable part includes even the "small vibration" resulting therefrom, which is called thought, or the "immortal" soul.

The other, nonperishable and microscopic part, which has been transmitted from generation to generation since the beginning of the world, is the *germ.*

The germ is that God in two persons, that God born of the union of the two most infinitesimal of living things, the *half-cells* known as the Spermatozoon and the Ovum.

Both inhabit abysses of night and hazy red, in the midst of streams — our blood — which bear globules spaced apart like planets.

There are eighteen million queens, the female half-cells, waiting in the depths of their cavern.

They penetrate and govern worlds with their glance. They are perfect goddesses. For them, no physical laws obtain — they disobey the law of gravitation. To the universal attraction of the scientists they oppose affinities proper unto themselves. Nothing exists for them but what they wish.

In other, equally formidable, chasms, they are there, the millions of gods in whom resides the Power, and who created Adam on the first day.

When the god and the goddess wish to unite, they bring with them, each from his own side, the one toward the other, the world they inhabit. Men and women think they choose each other... as though the earth should boast of revolving on purpose!

It is this passive inevitability, as of a falling stone, which men and women call love.

The god and goddess are about to unite... In order to meet, they need a length of time which, according to human measurements, varies between a second and two hours...

Yet a little longer, and another world will be created, a little, pale-coral Buddha, hiding its eyes, which are so dazzled by their proximity to the absolute that they have never opened, hiding its eyes behind its little, starlike hand...

Then the man and the woman awake and mount up to the heavens, crushing the gods like vermin.

Man, on that day, is called Titan, or Malthus.

9

THE INDIAN SO CELEBRATED
BY THEOPHRASTUS

Access to the hall was through a double door.

The "Indian" opened the first door, closing it behind him. He heard the bolt slip on the other side, drawn by Bathybius, to be opened only twenty-four hours later. On his own side of the door he drew the inside bolt, and stretched out his arms toward the second door...

It had opened while his back had been turned, and he recognized, leaning against the doorjamb, all pink and naked, and seemingly transparent in the lamplight, the smiling Ellen Elson.

With his beard, his pince-nez, and his conventional garments, Marcueil had divested himself of all remembrance of the world.

All that remained were a man and a woman, free, face to face, for eternity.

Twenty-four hours, was that not an eternity for a man who claimed that no number had any importance?

It was the *alone at last* of a man and a woman renouncing everything in order to be cloistered in each other's arms.

"Is it possible?" sighed their mouths, and they said no more, for they united.

But a cold irony retained its grip on Marcueil who, though powdered with red-gold dust and made up like an Indian, was — as he suddenly recognized — as basically ridiculous as Marcueil, the man of the *world*.

"Alone at last!" he laughed sneeringly, pushing Ellen away. "And the seven harlots who'll be coming, and the doctor who'll be watching?"

Ellen laughed in turn, discordantly, like a drunken streetwalker, the most beautiful of all laughs.

"There are your women! There!" (she grabbed something off the bed and threw it like a blade at the "Indian's" breast) " — the key to your woman-safe! It's well locked! I'm keeping them for you, and they're in good hands. But they are mine, your women, because you are mine! *'How many are you?'* a barefoot little man, wrapped in a monk's robe, once asked me. It's simple enough: I AM SEVEN! Is that enough for you, my dear 'Indian'?"

"It's crazy!" said Marcueil who, with his predilection for infinites, seemed at the moment disposed to infinite coldness. "That doctor who's going to *see...* he'll recognize you."

"I've brought a mask," said Ellen.

"What an idea! Your driver's mask, as though lots of women wear them, and Miss Elson were not known as a driving enthusiast! Everyone has seen it. Bathybius will recognize you all the more easily, that's all."

"My masks are all pink, and this one is black!"

"That's a woman's reasoning."

"Does that mean it's worthless? Listen, it's one of your women's masks, four of them have one, it's the fashion... And besides... ah!... and besides, it's fine for a doctor! And also, one of your women's masks, that should please you, you'll imagine it's her you're embracing... and I shall imagine that I've cut her head off... And then... I'm not altogether a harlot, you wouldn't want me to be altogether naked!"

Her face disappeared behind the black velvet. Her eyes and teeth shone.

A second later a click was heard, and Bathybius' white hair vaguely frosted up the little windowpane at the end of the hall.

"Let's go, Indian," jested Ellen. "Science is watching us, Science with a capital S, or rather, since even that is not impressive enough, SCIENCE with a capital SCYTHE!"

Marcueil remained cold:

"After all, how do you know that I *am* the *Indian?* I shall be, perhaps... *afterward.*"

"I don't know," said Ellen, "I don't know anything. You will be and then you won't be... you will be *more* than the Indian."

"AND MORE," mused Marcueil. "What does that mean? It's like the fleeting shadow of that race... *And more,* that's something that is no longer fixed, it recedes beyond the infinite, it's the ungraspable, a phantom..."

"You were the Shadow," said Ellen.

And he took her in his arms, automatically, just to have some tangible support to hold on to.

They became aware of the fragrance of some of the

Perpetual Motion race roses, which were in a crystal vase on a table, still not faded.

Like a crown of laurels with its leaves quivering in the breeze, the name of the being who was to show that he was "beyond the Indian" hovered before Marcueil's eyes and then became clear:

"THE SUPERMALE."

The clock announced that it was midnight, and Ellen listened to its strokes.

"Has it finished? Well, then... it's your move, dear Master."

And they fell toward each other, their teeth rang, and the hollows of their chests — so absolutely were they the same height — clung together by suction and then rang out like a shot.

They began to make love, and it was like the departure of a distant expedition, of a great nuptial journey traversing not cities but all Love.

When first they came together Ellen could scarcely repress a cry, and her face contracted. To stifle her acute suffering she needed something to bite, and she chose the Indian's lip. Marcueil had been right in saying that for certain men all women are virgins, and Ellen suffered in proof of it, but she did not cry out, although she was hurt.

They both drew back at the very moment that others cling most closely together, for both were thinking of themselves alone, and had no wish to prepare other lives.

What is the use, when one is young? That is the sort of precaution to take — or stop taking — at the extreme of old age, when one has made one's will and is on one's deathbed.

The second embrace, more sharply savored, was like the rereading of a favorite book.

Only after several could Ellen discern some pleasure deep in the cold, glittering eyes of the "Indian"... she seemed to understand that he was happy because she was happy to the point of suffering.

"Sadist!" she said.

Marcueil broke into candid laughter. He was not the sort to beat women. Something in him was already too cruel for them, without his needing to add to it.

They continued, and each embrace was a port of call in a different land where they always discovered something, and always something better.

Ellen seemed decided to be happy a little oftener than her lover, and to reach the goal indicated by Theophrastus before him.

The "Indian" deepened in her the sources of anguished pleasure that no lover had ever even lightly touched.

At TEN, she sprang lightly out of the bed and returned bearing a dainty tortoise-shell box which she had taken from the top of the dresser.

"At TEN, you said, dear Master, one must dress the wounds with certain balms... This is an excellent balm distilled in Palestine..."

"Yes, *the shadow was creaking,*" murmured Marcueil. He corrected her gently: "At ELEVEN. Later."

"Right away," said Ellen.

The limits of human capacity were passed in the same way as the familiar landscape of a suburb is seen to disappear from a train window.

Ellen revealed herself an expert courtesan, but it was so natural! The "Indian" felt to her so like some idol carved from unknown and pure materials that whatever part of him she caressed seemed the purest.

For the rest of the night and the whole of the morning, the lovers had no hour of rest or refreshment; they dozed or kept awake, they couldn't have told which, they nibbled at cakes and cold dishes; and they drank — from the same goblet — which was but another of the thousand variations of their embrace.

At noon — the Indian had nearly reached, and Ellen had long since gone beyond, the figure set by Theophrastus — Ellen began to complain a little.

"I'm so hot!" she said, walking around the room, her hands on her distended breasts. "I'm not naked enough. Couldn't I take this thing off my face?"

The doctor's eyes were spying from behind his windowpane.

"When shall we take it off?" repeated Ellen.

"When the rings around your eyes extend beyond the mask," said Marcueil.

"Let that be soon," moaned Ellen.

He took her in his arms, where she remained limply folded like a crumpled-up scarf, and put her back to bed like a child, straightening her out, drawing the bearskin

over her feet, and talking to her with comic pedantry to
make her laugh:

"Aristotle says in his *Problems:* Why is it not helpful in
love to have cold feet?"

Then he recited some of Florian's fables:

> "A little monkey gathered
> A nut in its green shell..."

Suddenly they realized that they were hungry.

They threw themselves on the table laden in
Gargantuan fashion, and ate like poor people in a soup
kitchen, poor people with their guts hollowed out by apéri-
tifs designed for billionaires.

The "Indian" consumed all the red meats and Ellen all
the pastries, but he did not drink all the champagne, as the
woman took for herself the foam of the first glass from each
bottle. She bit into it as though crunching meringues.

Then she embraced her lover, so that on top of his red
make-up he was coated with sugary substances all over his
body.

Later they made love twice... They had plenty of time,
it was not yet two in the afternoon.

Then they slept, and were still sleeping like the dead at
eleven twenty-seven that evening.

The doctor, his head nodding, and ready to fall asleep
himself, inscribed the total so far reached:

70

and put away his fountain pen.

Theophrastus' figure had been equaled, but not surpassed.

At eleven twenty-eight Marcueil awoke, or rather that part of him that constituted the *Indian* had awakened before him.

Under his embrace, Ellen cried out in pain, rose, slightly staggering, one hand at her throat and the other on her genitals, her eyes ferreted about her like those of a sick man looking for his medicine or an ether addict looking for his Lethe...

Then she fell back on the bed. Through her clenched teeth her breath made the same imperceptible bubbling sound that is made by crabs, creatures who, perhaps, hum what they try to remember of the Sirens' song...

Her body still seeking to escape the intensity of its burning, her mouth yet found the "Indian's" mouth...

And she remembered no more pain.

They had thirty minutes left before midnight, enough time for them to live once more counting what had gone before, through what had previously been considered the limits of human forces...

82

wrote Bathybius.

When they had finished, Ellen sat up, arranged her hair, and stared at her lover with hostile eyes.

"That wasn't the least bit funny," she said.

The man picked up a fan, half opened it, and then, taking a swing, slapped her face with it.

The woman jumped, drew from her hair a long, sword-shaped pin and, vengeance-bent, aimed it at Marcueil's eyes, which were shining on a level with her own.

Marcueil allowed his force to act: his eyes protected themselves.

Under their hypnotic gaze the woman lowered her weapon and immediately fell into a cataleptic sleep.

Her arm with the projecting steel remained horizontal.

Then Marcueil placed his forefinger between Ellen's eyes and at once woke her, for it was time.

WHO ART THOU, HUMAN CREATURE?

A miserable little tinkle, like the tip of a crutch scraping on a sidewalk; a miserable little tinkling thing, midnight, exhausted its twelve strokes in the decrepit Lurance clock tower.

This earthly sound revived Ellen, who had been beginning to doze again, this time in a natural slumber. She counted each tearful chime.

"Ha, ha, *human forces!*" she laughed sardonically, a bit disgruntled at being disturbed by so insignificant an intrusion. Then she doubled up with laughter and laughed herself back to sleep.

The door opened.

The doctor was framed in the doorway.

Bathybius stood swaying for a few seconds, benumbed by the odor of love, and blinded by the uniform whiteness of the electric lights glaring all over the immense hall, like the candles on an altar bedecked for some prodigious marriage rite.

The masked woman, her breasts erect, her fingers and toes crooked and slightly trembling, her laughter, in her sleep, turning into a very soft death rattle, lay sprawled across the bearskin...

The scarlet, naked, muscular, and obscene figure of the "Indian" bounded toward this clothed, hoary, and ape-bearded creature who was coming into the room without realizing what sort of a boundary he was crossing.

And the Supermale, roaring like a beast disturbed in its lair, saluted Bathybius with the same words (because there were no others to be said) with which the genie in the *Thousand and One Nights* greets the Vizier's ambassador: "Who art thou, human creature?"

The galleries were swarming with people and, at the end of the farthest drawing room, tiny men, playing instruments, were chirping like crickets in a box.

AND MORE

The naked, vermilioned "Indian" was carried off into the waiting throng and acclaimed as if he were a champion, an actor, or a king.

At the far end of the illuminated series of salons, bows were energetically striking strings to produce something like the *Te Deum* of exasperated love.

A black suit, flowering with a bed of exuberant and unkempt decorations — for, like a weed, the Agricultural Merit Medal appeared among them — hastened toward Marcueil who, secure behind his false Redskin's epidermis, recognized Saint-Jurieu.

"Depopulation is now but an empty word," sniveled the senator in admiration.

"Hardly even a word," sang out the general.

"Our country can count on a hundred more defenders every day," they all exclaimed together.

"Only eighty-two," corrected Bathybius, stammering. "But if the 'Indian' deigns to take the trouble, it can be, in twenty-four hours, and only at the rate of SIX per hour: a hundred and forty-four!"

"A gross," commented Saint-Jurieu.

"And this number can be multiplied to almost any extent by artificial insemination," continued the doctor, getting excited. "And that even without the presence of..."

"The author whose editor you are, dear doctor!" jested some voices.

"I should like to reserve a special edition," said the cynical voice of Henriette Cyne, who had come in, no one knew how.

The "Indian," in reply to all these speeches, gestured with a tranquil motion of his head:

"No."

"What's he saying?" muttered the general. "That he can't have children? Well who can, then?"

The "Indian," still impassive and taciturn, cast a glance about the room, raised his index finger and placed it on the constellated chest of Saint-Jurieu.

"It's always those who can't who try," interpreted Henriette Cyne philosophically.

And the "Indian" slipped off, fearful that Ellen's incognito might not be respected. He ran into the hall, closing the door behind him.

Scarcely had he entered than a supple body, still warm from his embrace, wrapped itself about him and pushed him onto the bed of fur.

And the young woman's breath murmured, in a kiss that made his ears buzz:

"At last we're through with the betting to please... Mr. Theophrastus! Now let's think of ourselves. *We haven't yet made love... for pleasure!*"

She had double-bolted the door.

Suddenly, near the ceiling, a windowpane shattered, and the glass showered down on the rug.

O SWEETEST NIGHTINGALE

It was at that moment that the women broke through the glass panel. The fragments tinkled as they began to fall, and then were absorbed by the hair of the rug which swallowed up the sound, as when a burst of laughter, conscious of its own false note, interrupts itself.

The women did not try to laugh right off.

Finally Virginie said: "Hey, you lovers!"

"Haven't you finished yet, since the day before yesterday?" asked Irène.

"They say themselves that they haven't begun yet," laughed Eupure sardonically.

"Were you waiting for us?" said Modeste.

They were bunched together behind the iron frame, but André and Ellen could only see the upper parts of their faces.

"Isn't there some way to keep them quiet?" growled the Supermale. "Hide yourself," he ordered Ellen.

"I don't care if they see us, so long as all they show you is their faces," said Ellen. "I wear my mask a different way."

Like a Majesty proudly opening the unique casket containing the royal diamonds, she pulled open the Indian's arms which, encircling her, were concealing a little of her shoulders.

Then she made the gesture that is permitted only to sovereigns: she knelt before the man.

Only those girls who are born to be servants think themselves obliged to redeem their services by increasing their fees.

Ellen caressed Marcueil passionately. Vexed that he was not yet altogether spent, her mouth bit him repeatedly. It must be that he did not love his mistress, since he had not yet given her all, given until he could give no more!

The Indian experienced ecstasy several times, sometimes passive like a man, sometimes like a woman...

This, to be sure, was what Theophrastus had meant by: "And more."

The girls' imprecations floated above them like a canopy.

Amused at first, they were getting exasperated. Marcueil sat up, seized a light Japanese vase and made as if to throw it at the window. But he changed his mind: he was not in his own home, since he was the *Indian.*

"Still, I must make some sort of noise to make them be quiet," he said. "Oh! if only I had a hunting horn!"

His eyes searched over the large, encumbered table on which he had replaced the vase.

And suddenly, with the abrupt decisiveness of a man under attack loading a revolver, he took a cylindrical object from the drawer.

Above him the voices began to sound frightened.

"No funny business, Mr. Savage," cried Virginie, who could not quit the breach, as she had been the first to arrive and was now hemmed in by her companions.

"Don't be afraid," jested Ellen, grabbing André with a gesture of tragic effrontery. "Don't be afraid, ladies, I have hold of him!"

André freed himself and shrugged his shoulders. He seemed to be winding with a key a sort of box topped by a crystal corolla, the one into which the bouquet of roses had been thrust, without water. It appeared to be leaning at an angle simply because of the weight of the flowers. A phonograph loudspeaker occupied the center of the table from which they had eaten. From its horn, now strangely blocked by odors and colors, there blared forth a loud singing that filled the hall.

"Bravo," said Virginie again.

The word was inaudible, but the gesture of her pudgy hands could be seen as they tried, ironically, to applaud, without relinquishing their grip on her vantage point.

"Why don't you —" and she shouted at the top of her voice in an effort to be heard above the organlike roar of the enormous instrument — "show motion pictures?"

The girls' lips were moving, but their voices could no longer be heard.

Whether or not they heard Virginie, André and Ellen seemed disposed to answer her request by striking some theatrical attitudes: the "Indian" had plucked a red rose from the bouquet and offered it, with a tenderness humorously tinged with ceremony, to the masked woman on the divan; then their mouths joined for a minute, with no more concern for their audience, who were now unable to trouble them, and let themselves sway to the flowing rhythm of the music.

André had slipped the first roll he came across into the phonograph; and when he came back to Ellen's side, to place on her youthful ivory flesh the vermilion rose that seemed like a scrap torn from his Redskin's mouth-colored epidermis, the instrument struck up an old ballad.

Although André Marcueil was not unaware that the song was very well known, and appeared in several anthologies of folk songs, he shuddered disagreeably at the curious coincidence of his gesture with the first few verses:

> I picked a crimson ro-se
> To offer to my love,
> O sweetest nightingale!

Ellen uttered a cry, hid her head beneath Marcueil's arm, then raised it again and looked into her lover's eyes with a glance that clearly signified, in spite of her mask:

"What an extraordinary thing, but as it was you who did it, it doesn't surprise me any more."

André was now master of himself once more and dissimulating his concern; she broke into joyous laughter, but a second rapid glance at Marcueil's expression revealed a cloud that she thought she could account for.

"You're not going to be jealous, are you, at that glass mouth presuming to offer me flowers? He was quite in

order, my dear, they did belong to him. He's giving you a
lesson in gallantry."

And, as she knew some rather improper words, she
specified: "The *paying-poker,* isn't that right, isn't that the
expression?" The instrument, meanwhile, had repeated:

>   I picked a crimson ro-se
>   To offer to my love,

Then it gave a sort of macabre trill, an interminable
krr... as though chiding the young woman for her famil-
iarity, or else clearing its throat; but this was merely a pause
before the second couplet:

>   The rose brings grievous news, love,
>   Grievous beyond all telling.
>   O sweetest nightingale!
>   The rose brings grievous news, love,
>   Grievous beyond all telling.

The crystal funnel vibrated, drawing out the last two
syllables like a dying call:

"*El-len!*"

Set amidst the rest of the flowers, it looked like an
oversized monocle for a nasty-tempered cyclops, which was
staring at them, or like a highwayman's blunderbuss on the
main road of their love, or, even worse, like a flower in the
buttonhole of a very dapper old gentleman, blooming with
a whole store of bleeding things which, too, were going to
constitute "grievous news."

> At the first figure of the dance
> The fair maid's color changed,
>   O sweetest nightingale!

"At the first?" said Ellen, whose color did indeed change, as she blushed. "This vase was a little late in getting the rose stalks out of its eye, if it's only just noticed us..."

"A single figure, it has to be the first one," said the "Indian."

Ellen did not answer, for they were making love.

The old gentleman with the crystal monocle was a far more indiscreet viewer than Bathybius, for he began again — without a pause, and apparently still observing them — in his halting voice:

> ...gale,
> Hay, hay, hay, hay, hay, hay...
> Krrr...
> At the first figure of the dance
> The fair maid's color changed.

He had an extremely comical, indrawn, and sudden way of attacking "cha-a-anged," midway between a hiccup and a sob.

Then he went: *krrr...* and waited, like a simple Bathybius. He had imposed an unbroken silence upon the women above and, his monocle trembling slightly, he continued. Neither André nor Ellen found this monocle in bloom more absurd than anything else, whether human or superhuman:

At the next figure of the dance...

Without further prompting, and as though by erotic suggestion, hypnotized, André and Ellen obeyed.

> The fair maid changed aga-in,
> O sweetest nightingale!
> Hay... hay... hay...
> At the next figure of the dance
> The fair maid changed aga-in

When the flowered being went *krr,* Ellen's head fell back, and she made a little rattling sound that was not a lover's moan; the Supermale felt his own head swimming, stirring up associations of insane ideas and unfamiliar words.

"I'm a bit drunk," murmured Ellen. "It hurts so!"

And in the midst of all this madness he understood, in a lucid flash, that if he did not silence, as he had silenced the women, and immediately, over there on the table, that imperious voice that was now master of his hyperesthetized senses, of his spine, and very nearly of his brain, he would have to possess again, and his member would be unable *not* to possess, the dying woman whom his arms had not yet released.

He would have liked to kill her now, to stab her, so as not to be forced to make her suffer otherwise. Her eyes were closed, and a little tear half opened them to make its way out, moistening the sidepiece of her mask. One would have said that it was the mask that was weeping. Her breasts were erect in a joy or a suffering that was no longer terrestrial. André wanted to get up, to stop, or break the phonograph, to seize the vase and smash its glass horn. He noticed, and was surprised that he hadn't remembered them earlier, within reach of his arm, by the bed, the accessories of his cast-off, comic-opera "Indian's" clothing. He threw the tomahawk which, naturally enough, he didn't know how to throw, and it hit the back of the chair with its noncutting edge, showing contempt for all Fenimore Cooper's tales. Next he threw one of Ellen's slippers, which was a more deadly weapon; it struck the edge of the crystal corolla, which vibrated, without either breaking or being upset, and it also swept away all the last roses, which fell to the ground. Everything that we have just taken such a long time to describe happened while the two notes *la* and *so,* which corresponded to the two syllables of *mo-ore,* were being played.

The horn of the phonograph looked like the shining, menacing throat of a snake, no longer hidden beneath the flowers, and André, under the spell, had to obey the order. His member, like himself, also had to obey the order; the monster ordered, in a limpid and piercing voice:

> At the third figure of the dance
> The fair maid fell down dead,
>   O sweetest nightingale!
> At the third figure of the dance
> The fair maid fell down de...

André didn't hear the final hiccup: a tremendous, high-pitched cry, made up of seven cries, had burst from the women's gallery, where the faces suddenly abandoned the window. The spell was broken, and André got up, without having followed the maniac impulse through to the end... The phonograph gave a final *krr* and stopped. It was just like the release of an alarm clock, although it was not the end of a dream. The cold, blue dawn of the second day that they had been there let its shroud fall, from the tall windows of the hall, onto the divan. Ellen was no longer breathing, her heart was no longer beating, her feet and hands were as glacial as the dawn.

A new flood of baroque memories came chattering into the Supermale's troubled brain:

" 'Why,' Aristotle asks in his *Problems,* 'is it not of assistance to the sexual act to have cold feet?'"

Then he guffawed, in spite of himself, though an obscure self whispered to him that he had every reason to weep. Then he wept, although another self, which seemed to nourish a personal hatred toward the previous one, explained to him at length, even though in a single instant, that this was the time to roar with laughter. Next he rolled on the ground, the whole length of the hall. His naked body came into contact with a little, hairy, velvety rectangle on the stone floor. He thought he had gone mad, so astounded was he that the bearskin that served as a rug should seem so minute to him.

It was Ellen's mask, which had fallen off during her agony.

THE DISCOVERY OF WOMAN

Her mask had fallen...

Ellen was now quite naked.

Except for her mask, he had possessed her entirely for the last two days.

Without her mask, he had seen her frequently before those two days, but time is measured by the number of events that fill and distend it. The minute during which she had awaited him, all pink, her right arm raised, leaning against the doorjamb, must have been back in the beginning of time...

...In the days when something Superhuman created woman.

"Is it possible?" they used to say, in that past time.

Her mask had fallen, and it appeared absolutely clear to the Supermale that, although he had possessed Ellen entirely naked for the past two days, he had never really seen her, even without her mask.

He would never have seen her, if she had not been dead.

Prodigals usually turn miser at the very moment when they realize that their treasure has been squandered.

The Supermale would never see Ellen again, and her form was about to return, by the muscular contractions that precede decomposition, to what had existed before there was any form. He had never even wondered whether he had loved her, or whether she were beautiful.

The phrase from which their prodigious adventure had been born came back into his mind again, just as it had been when, choosing to be grotesque and vulgar, he had capriciously uttered it:

"The act of love is of no importance, since it can be performed indefinitely."

Indefinitely...

Yet there was an end.

An end to the Woman.

An end to Love.

"The Indian so celebrated by Theophrastus" fully knew that there would come an end to the woman, but he supposed that this pretty, fragile, and futile creature would give up voluptuousness if it were no longer the immediate goal, if it were only the means to a yet deeper and more heroic voluptuousness nearer to the limits of pain. He had put seven women in the gallery, in reserve, not otherwise than Arthur Gough would have brought seven spare automobiles... in case of a *breakdown*.

He laughed again, but wept nervously when he looked at Ellen.

She was very beautiful.

She had kept her promise: her mask had fallen, but

large circles had replaced it around her eyes! Other masks
were about to settle all over her, like flakes of purple snow:
the cadaverous, marmoreal veins that begin at the nostrils
and the belly.

The marble of life was still pure and luminous: at her
throat and her hips was the same imperceptible blight as on
freshly cut ivory.

Delicately raising his mistress's eyelids, Marcueil discovered that he had never seen the color of her eyes. They
were so dark as to defy all color, like the dark, dead leaves
at the bottom of the limpid Lurance moat, and they seemed
like two wells in her skull, sunk for the joy of seeing her
hair from the inside.

Her teeth were minute and well-kept toys. Death had
carefully closed up the two rows, like tiny, unspotted domi-
noes — too childish for counting to matter — in a child's
surprise box.

Her ears, there was no doubt, had been "hemmed" by
some lacemaker.

The tips of her breasts were curious, pink things,
which looked like each other, and like nothing else.

Her genitals seemed like a small, eminently stupid animal, as stupid as a shellfish — really, there was quite a
resemblance — but not less pink.

The Supermale perceived that he was engaged in discovering Woman, an exploration for which he had not
before had the leisure.

Assiduous lovemaking leaves no time to experience
love.

He kissed all his discoveries like rare gems with which

he would soon be obliged to part forever.

He kissed them — a thing he had not previously thought of doing, imagining that it would be evidence of a momentary impotence where more virile caresses were concerned — he kissed them to thank them for his discovery of them; he nearly thought: for his having invented them.

And he began to sink softly down beside his companion, who was asleep in the absolute, just as the first man had awoken near Eve and thought that she had come out of his side because she was beside him, in his quite natural surprise at finding the first woman whom love had made to blossom, in the place where some still anthropoid female had slept before.

He murmured her name, the meaning of which he now understood for the first time:

"Helen, Helen!"

"Helen, Helen!" sang melodiously through his brain, as though the phonograph were still playing and imposing its rhythm.

And Marcueil perceived that at this stage of his spent energies, when another man would have been fatigued, he was becoming sentimental. This was his transformation of the *post coitum animal triste.* Just as love had been restful for his legs, by a similar equilibrium his brain, in its turn, wanted to become active. And, just to send himself asleep, he composed some verses.

A naked woman, arms outstretched, the fount
Of all desire, saying: Can it be?
Eyes aflame with ineffable ecstasy —
The carats of this diamond, who can count?

Arms weakening as embrace succeeds embrace,
Another's body pliant to my assault,
Great, candid eyes, deceiving with such grace —
"I shall drink your tears — but make them less salt."

At the spasm she starts up, comatose,
A sweet pillow in which there beats a heart;
But sweetest of all, her loving mouth glows —
Her mouth, summit of Aphrodite's art.

Our mouths must form but one single alcove,
As you might join two cages door to door
For two wild beasts to consummate their love —
Our tongues thus bride and groom for ever more.

Like Adam, by a double breath inspired,
Awaking, finds that Eve is by his side,
I wake, and find my Queen so long desired —
Helen — eternal beauty — is my bride.

From the depths of time, an echoing horn sighed:

"Helen,
The plain
Of Hellen
Is wholly
Eros.

"To destroy
Troy
Is deployed
The pride
Of Argos.

"The skilled
Achill'
Despoils
The soil
Where Priam
Pleads."

The track of his chariot, which drags, obscene,
The corpse of Hector round the Trojan walls,
Enframes a gleaming mirror, in which Queen
Helen, naked, as her hair softly falls —

Queen Helen —
Preens
Herself.

"Helen,
The plain
Of Hellen
Is wholly
Love."

Old Priam pleads from his tower above:

"Achilles, Achilles, remorseless foe,
Your heart's harder than iron, than brass, than gold —

Harder, Achilles, than those walls below,
Harder than all our rough Trojan walls!"

At her mirror, the Queen preens herself:

"Oh no, Priam, nothing is so hard
As these ivory bucklers — Helen's breasts;
Their coral points quickened by wounds and blood,
Like seagull's eyes, encased in hard, white, downy nests:
Cold irises surround their scarlet soul's regard.
No, no, no, Priam — nothing is so hard."

Paris, sly foe
On Achill' steals
Like Cupid, with bow —
Arrows his heel;

Paris-Eros
So blond and so rose,
Handsome Paris, destroyer of peace,
Goddesses' judge, yet lover of women;
The ravisher of Helen of Greece,
Son of Priam,
Paris, the bowman, is laid bare:
Over his wild traces exults a chariot of war,
The vultures feed on his sex and on his dead eyes:

"Helen,
The plain
Of Hellen
Is wholly
Love."

Fate, Fate, oh cruel, too cruel Fate!
You drink the blood of mortals with foul joy:
Brave Hellenic bodies bestrew the plain of Troy,
Fate and vultures the same feast arrogate.
Too cruel Fate! Fate — the gods' hard forbear!

But Helen, opening her, lovely, limpid eyes:

"Fate is but a word — there is nothing in the skies —
If ever, than my eyes, other skies there were.
Mortals, do not pale; dare to scrutinize
My eyes' blue abyss; see mirrored there the slain.
Menelaus, Paris, they are both dead,
Husband and lover — and the dead bestrew the plain
To make a softer carpet to my tread,
A carpet of love, quivering beneath the prize;
And then, I often dress myself in green,

"And...I don't know...these days I have grown fond
of red."

"Helen is dead," repeated "the Indian so celebrated by
Theophrastus" through his sleep. "What remains of her for
me? The memory of her grace, her light, delicate, and perfumed memory, her floating and delicious living image,
almost more delicious than her living form itself. For I am
sure she will never leave me, and it is only the desire for an
unattainable eternity that obsesses and spoils the ephemeral
joys of lovers. Her memory will be a featherweight trophy
that I shall always carry with me, a precious phantom whose
undulating and fluid form, like a voluptuous hydra, bathes

my head and my groin with the caress of its tentacles.
Indian, so celebrated by Theophrastus, thou shalt always
carry with thee her slightly bloodied memory, so perfumed
and light and floating; thou shalt carry, like a scalp-hunting
Indian... *her hair!*"

And from the depths of the being of this man, who was
so abnormal that he could only warm his heart on the ice of
a corpse, arose the admission of this certainty, torn from
him by force:

"I adore her."

THE LOVE MACHINE

When Marcueil said: "I adore her," Ellen was no longer at his side.

Ellen was not dead.

Only fainted, in a swoon; women never die from this sort of adventure.

Her father greeted the return of his ill, drunk, happy, and cynical daughter with stupefaction, and Bathybius, summoned in haste, in spite of the woman's mask and without regard for professional secrecy or even professional prejudice — Bathybius added his confirmation:

"I saw it — as truly as though I had held it under a microscope or a speculum — I saw it face to face: the Impossible!"

But when the doxies were freed they spoke out, and their jealousy claimed its revenge.

Virginie called on Elson — beautiful, miraculously made up, with her pure forehead and her candid eyes, looking like Truth incarnate — and declared:

"The doctor is an old fool. We were there all the time. Nothing extraordinary happened. By the second day they still hadn't done anything, and when we were watching them they did it three times just to impress us, and then the woman wouldn't go on."

All that could be gotten out of Ellen was:

"I love him."

"Does he love you?" asked her father.

However much the Supermale had dishonored him, the American had but one outcome in view: André Marcueil must marry his daughter.

"I love him," was Ellen's reply to every question.

"Then he doesn't love you?" asked Elson.

This presumption largely determined the tragic course of the events that were to follow.

Bathybius was completely unnerved by what he had observed, and was instrumental in suggesting to William Elson the idea that: "He's not a man, he's a machine."

He added the old phrase he was always wont to repeat when speaking of Marcueil:

"The fellow just refuses to understand anything."

"He must love my daughter, though," reflected Elson who, although panic-stricken, remained practical, and was ready to demonstrate just how practical he was, even to the point of absurdity.

"Surely, doctor, science must be able to devise something!"

Bathybius' motley science could well have been compared to a compass with its needle gyrating like a pinwheel and coming to rest at random at any point but north. The physician's brain must have been more or less in the same state as the dynamometer that the Supermale had once demolished.

"The ancients had their philters," mused the chemist. "We should need to be able to rediscover processes, as old as human superstition, which force a soul to love!"

Arthur Gough was consulted, and said:

"There is suggestion... hypnotism... it's infallible, but that's the doctor's department."

Bathybius shuddered.

"I saw him put the woman to sleep... put her to sleep... *in articulo mortis...* just when she was about to jab his eyes out with a pin... His eyes would knock anyone right over... No one is mad enough, is he, to look into the eyes of the double headlights of a locomotive at night, which loom larger and larger as they bear down on him?"

"Well then," said Arthur Gough, "let's go back to the ancient processes. The Desert Fathers were acquainted with a machine that might possibly serve our purpose. It is described in Saint Jerome's *Life of St. Hilarion:*

"'Certainly thy strength, (O Demon) must be very great, as thou art thus bound and halted by a strip of copper and a braided wire!'"

"An electromagnetic device," said William Elson, without hesitation.

And thus it was that Arthur Gough, the engineer who could build anything, was called upon to create the most unusual machine of modern times, a machine not designed to produce a physical effect, but to act on forces hitherto considered out of reach: the machine-to-inspire-love.

If André Marcueil were a machine, or endowed with an iron constitution that enabled him to overcome machines, why then, the combined efforts of the engineer, the chemist, and the physician would pit one machine against another for the greater good of bourgeois science, medicine, and morality. Since this man had become a mechanism, the equilibrium of the world required that another mechanism should manufacture — a soul.

The construction of the device was simple enough for Arthur Gough. He gave no explanation to his two colleagues. It was all set up within two hours.

He based his experiment on one of Faraday's. When a piece of copper is dropped between the two poles of a powerful electromagnet, being of nonmagnetic metal it cannot be influenced; nevertheless it will not fall through. It will float down slowly as though a viscous liquid occupied the space between the magnetic poles. Now, if one is brave enough to place one's head in this spot — and Faraday, as we know, did carry out this experiment — absolutely nothing can be felt. What is remarkable is precisely that absolutely nothing is felt, but the terrible thing is that *nothing*, in scientific parlance, has never meant anything else than "the unknown," the unexpected force, x, perhaps death itself.

Another known fact on which the device was based is that in America criminals are generally electrocuted by a current of twenty-two hundred volts. Death is instantaneous, the body fries, and the convulsive paroxysms are frightful to the point of making it seem as though the device that has killed it is falling upon the corpse in an effort to revive it. Now, if a person be subjected to a current more than four times as strong — let's say ten thousand volts — *nothing happens.*

To elucidate what follows, let us note that the water running through the Lurance moat provided power for an eleven-thousand-volt dynamo.

André Marcueil, still plunged in a stupor, was tied to an armchair by his own servants — since servants will always obey a doctor if he diagnoses that their master is either ill or mad. His arms and legs were held spread-eagled by leather straps, and a strange object was placed on his skull, a sort of crenelated platinum crown with its teeth pointing downward. In the front and back it had a sort of tubular diamond. The crown was made in two sections, each provided with a red earpiece lined with a damp sponge to ensure contact with his temples on either side. The two metal semicircles were insulated from each other by a thick sheet of glass that projected over his forehead and occiput, and sparkled like rhinestones. Marcueil did not wake up when the springs of the sideplates were pressed hard against his temples, but it was at that instant that he dreamed of scalps and hair.

The doctor, Arthur Gough, and William Elson were observing, unseen from the neighboring room, and the patient with his crown, still undressed, and with his make-up peeling off in places, as the gilding wears off a statue, presented so inhuman a spectacle that the two Americans, who "knew their Gospels," needed a few moments to compose themselves and call on their common sense to shake off the pitiful and supernatural image of the King of the

Jews diademed with thorns and nailed on a cross.

Could they be on the track of a force that was capable of regenerating the world, or destroying it?

Wires encased in gutta-percha and green silk led to the electrodes and held the Supermale as though by a leash attached to his temples. They wound and dangled, passing through the wall like vermin gnawing an avenue of escape somewhere in the direction of the crackling and rumbling of the dynamo.

William Elson, a curious scientist and a practical parent, prepared to throw the current.

"One minute," said Arthur Gough.

"What is it?" asked the chemist.

"Although this device may produce the desired effect," said the engineer, "it may also yield nothing at all, or something quite different. Besides, it was made rather hastily."

"That's fine, it'll make this an experiment," interrupted Elson, pressing the switch.

André Marcueil did not budge.

He seemed to be feeling a rather pleasant sensation.

The three scientists, spying on him, gathered that Marcueil distinctly understood *what the machine required of him.* For at that very moment, still dreaming, he said:

"I adore her."

The machine was working, then, according to its builders' calculations, but an indescribable phenomenon occurred, one which should nevertheless have entered into their equations.

Everyone knows that when two electrodynamic machines are coupled together, the one with the higher output *charges* the other.

Within this antiphysical circuit connecting the nervous system of the Supermale to the eleven thousand volts, transformed perhaps into something that was no longer electricity, neither the chemist nor the doctor nor the engineer could deny the evidence: it was the man who was influencing the machine-to-inspire-love.

Thus, as might mathematically have been foreseen, if the machine really did produce love, it was THE MACHINE THAT FELL IN LOVE WITH THE MAN.

Arthur Gough, in a couple of leaps, was down inspecting the dynamo; horrified, he telephoned up that it was now receiving current and revolving backward at an unknown and astonishing speed.

"I should never have thought it possible... never... but it's really so natural!" murmured the doctor. "In these days when metal and machines are all-powerful, man, if he is to survive, must become stronger than the machines, just as he became stronger than the beasts... A mere adaptation to his environment... But this man is the first of a new race..."

Arthur Gough, however, with a mechanical gesture — he was, like the others, a practical man — Arthur Gough, so as not to waste this unexpected energy, linked up the dynamo with a group of accumulators...

When he got back upstairs he was faced with a terrible sight. Either it was that the Supermale's nervous tension had reached too fabulous a potential, or, on the contrary, that it had grown weaker (perhaps because he was beginning to wake up) and the previously overcharged accumulators had grown stronger and reversed the flow of the current, or there was perhaps quite a different cause, but the platinum crown grew first red- and then white-hot.

In a painful paroxysm of effort, Marcueil snapped the straps holding his forearms and raised his hands to his head. His crown — probably owing to its faulty construction, with which Elson later bitterly reproached Arthur Gough — its glass plate not being sufficiently thick, or else too easily fusible — his crown collapsed inward, then folded in two.

Drops of molten glass flowed like tears down the Supermale's cheeks.

On contact with the floor, several exploded violently, like Prince Rupert's drops.

We know that glass, when liquefied and tempered under certain conditions — here by the acidulated water of the contact sponges — resolves into explosive drops.

The three hidden spectators distinctly saw the crown totter, and, like a pair of incandescent jaws, sink its teeth into the man's temples. Marcueil howled and sprang forward, bursting his remaining bonds and tearing out the electrodes, whose ends were sputtering behind him.

Marcueil bounded down the stairs... The three men understood how lamentably tragic can be a dog with a pot tied to its tail.

When they reached the steps, all they could see was a grimacing, pain-racked silhouette rushing at superhuman speed down the driveway, then grasping the gate with a grip of steel, with no other purpose than to flee or to struggle, twisting two of the square bars of the monumental grille.

Meanwhile, in the vestibule, the broken wires writhed and hissed, electrocuting a servant who had tried to run past them, and setting fire to an arras which was consumed without a flame, with sullen slowness, seemingly swallowed up by a vast red lip.

And André Marcueil's body, stark naked, and gilded in spots with reddish gold, remained wrapped around the bars — or the bars remained wrapped around it...

There the Supermale died, twisted into the ironwork.

. .   . .

Ellen Elson is cured, and married.

She imposed only one condition before she accepted a husband: that he be capable of containing his love within the prudent bounds of human capacities...

Finding him was... "just a game."

She found an adroit jeweler to set, in the place of a pearl in a ring that she faithfully wears, one of the solid tears of the Supermale.

E N D

Selected Exact Change Titles

GUILLAUME APOLLINAIRE
The Heresiarch & Co.

✳

The Poet Assassinated

LOUIS ARAGON
Paris Peasant

✳

The Adventures of Telemachus

ANTONIN ARTAUD
Watchfiends & Rack Screams

JOHN CAGE
Composition in Retrospect

LEONORA CARRINGTON
The Hearing Trumpet

SALVADOR DALÍ
Oui

GIORGIO DE CHIRICO
Hebdomeros

ALICE JAMES
The Death and Letters
of Alice James

ALFRED JARRY
Exploits & Opinions of
Dr. Faustroll, Pataphysician

FRANZ KAFKA
The Blue Octavo Notebooks

LAUTRÉAMONT
Maldoror

GÉRARD DE NERVAL
Aurélia

FERNANDO PESSOA
The Book of Disquiet

JEROME ROTHENBERG, ED.
Revolution of the Word

RAYMOND ROUSSEL
How I Wrote Certain of My Books

PHILIPPE SOUPAULT
Last Nights of Paris

GERTRUDE STEIN
Everybody's Autobiography

STEFAN THEMERSON
Bayamus & Cardinal Pölätüo

DENTON WELCH
In Youth is Pleasure

✳

A Voice Through a Cloud

EXACT CHANGE 5 BREWSTER ST. CAMBRIDGE MA 02138
WWW.EXACTCHANGE.COM